THE ZOOM SITUATION

SPACE COCAINE

THE ZOOM
SITUATION

contents

Whispers

Erik Grove

The delivery guy shook the security gate in front of the house. "Hello?"

A fat red laser lit up his chest.

"What the . . ?" He stumbled three steps back.

"Still yourself, Earthling!" a distorted voice barked at him. Ness had to mute her mic to keep from breaking character with a laugh when the delivery guy's eyes opened so wide she thought they might explode. She piloted the drone into view.

"Fuck all of this." The delivery guy—the app said his name was Gabe—headed back to his car, a mint green sedan that still had Ness's Funyons.

"Hey, hold on," Ness said through the drone's speaker. She took the filter off her voice. "I'm just kidding around."

Gabe scratched the top of his head with a blue-gloved finger. "Really taking the pandemic crazy to a new level, huh?"

"Can you just leave my stuff at the gate please?" Ness popped a hand out from the drone's belly and waved.

"Damn." He eyed the drone. "You find that on the internet?"

"It's custom."

Gabe nodded and went to the trunk of the car. He took out several bags and put them down. "You know, I could take these up to your door like a normal if you opened up your gate."

"Not an option, sport," Ness said. "Heavy security. Hush hush. CIA wet works. No questions."

"Sure." Gabe did not seem remotely convinced. "Well, you keep having whatever kind of strange fucking rich person day you're having in there."

"Wait."

Gabe sighed. "This is going to get weirder isn't it?"

"No . . . Maybe. I have questions."

"I don't have COVID, lady. I wore gloves at the store. I have a mask and hand sanitizer. So much hand sanitizer. I put that shit on my cereal. I swear."

"Not about that," Ness told him.

"Um?"

"You're a gig worker right?"

". . . Yeah."

"That means you sign up to the thing and it just gives you little jobs and stuff?"

"That's the general idea. Late-stage capitalism is a real fun time."

"Where do you live?"

He didn't answer that but instead stuck his hands in his pockets.

"Not specifically," Ness clarified. "I'm not a serial killer. I mean, like where in the valley?"

"Sure. Why not?" Gabe said. "Serial killers never lie about being serial killers because that would be unethical. I'm over in Echo Park."

"That's pretty close," Ness said. "You want a job? Doing things for me? Exclusively?"

"Is this is some real LA shit? Do you want me to fuck a mannequin while you take a bath in milk or something?"

"I . . . Have people tried to get you to do that?"

"I'd rather not talk about it." From Gabe's facial expression, largely concealed beneath a mask, she couldn't tell if he was joking or not.

"Well, I don't want you to do any of that. Just picking up stuff for me. Groceries. Prescriptions. Regular things."

"You want me to get you groceries?" Gabe nodded at the bags in front of the gate. "Like I just did?"

"Exclusively," Ness said. "I would pay you. A lot."

"What's a lot?"

"Well, do you have a student loans?"

Gabe nodded.

"I could probably fix that."

"I got an assistant," Ness told Viv. They were talking with Wisper, Ness's prototype super secure video conferencing app. Like Zoom but absolutely no uninvited hairy dangly bits.

Viv looked at something out of view of the computer camera. Multitasking. Love in the time of COVID. "Oh? You called one of those agencies I sent you?"

"Sort of. His name is Gabe. He plays video games with me. Online obviously."

Viv turned from her second monitor. "Is he twelve?"

"No. Maybe? He can drive. When do they give you a license for that?"

"Are you twelve?"

Ness stuck her tongue out.

Viv sighed. "Well, I'm glad," she said finally, simply.

Ness nodded. "I'm growing as a person. How's the LSD Teletubby conversation?"

Viv clicked a key. Warbled oddly pitched baby talk mixed with static came through Ness's speakers. Viv frowned. "About where I was."

Ness was smarter than most people on the planet. That wasn't arrogance. It was verifiable. There were studies and she had a coffee cup that said so. But Viv was a different kind of smart. Her LSD Teletubby babble was a conversation she had initiated with the cosmos. Her theory was that all the weird electromagnetic static that most physicists dismissed as cosmic microwave background radiation left over from the Big Bang was not that at all but rather a signal from someone. Maybe aliens. Maybe God. Maybe Jupiter's snotty kid brother that got kicked out of the Milky Way for fighting with Saturn all the time. It was a bonkers theory more science fiction than Scientific American but Viv had done the work and Ness had little doubt that she would crack it.

"Shitty," Ness said. "Maybe check the baseline equations?"

"Or it could be the translation software," Viv suggested.

Now Viv was trolling. "It's not the software, babe. The developer is pretty hot shit."

Viv leaned forward. She rubbed her eyes. She didn't look good. Pale. Wrung out like a rag from a bucket of bleach water. They specifically did not live together. It was a whole thing that Ness wanted to avoid talking about for forever. Viv had her work at the lab and with the pandemic and everything they decided it would be better to make their relationship virtual for a while. That was another whole thing that Ness wanted to avoid talking about.

"So, are you eating and stuff?" Ness asked Viv. She managed to distill all of her feelings about the world and their relationship and all of her fears into a single question. She'd always been an efficient coder.

Viv's nose wrinkled. "What happened to the romancing mood?"

"Hashtag 2020," Ness said. "And you were workaholing anyway. How's your blood sugar?"

"It's fine. I'm just . . . You know."

Fine was not the answer Ness was hoping for. Fine meant that Viv probably wasn't checking her blood sugar which was incredibly stupid and yeah, Ness knew how crunch mode worked, but Ness was also stupid. They both sucked at basic human being upkeep. It was one of their cute couple things. Ness had tried to convince Viv to get one of those automatic monitors with an insulin pump, but Viv bristled at the idea of her blood sugar readings being hacked and analyzed by Ness. Ness couldn't really defend herself from that as she would absolutely hack a blood sugar monitor.

"Did you get some fresh air today?" Viv asked, girlfriend Judo reversal.

"HVAC, babe," Ness said. "It circulates."

"Sunlight, Ness. Vitamin D."

"Gabe brought me vitamins." Ness grabbed the bottle. She shook them for the camera. "So."

"You could try going out onto the back deck maybe?"

Ness smiled but she wasn't feeling smile she was feeling fuck off. "Maybe." Ness made the word colder than Antartica.

"Alright, so, mom time finished obviously," Viv said. "Did you talk to Grams?"

"I did," Ness smiled. "Got her all set up on Wisper."

"So, she survived the interrogation?"

Viv meant the security setup. "She complained about it constantly," Ness said. "Said I was paranoid."

"You are paranoid."

Ness tensed. She didn't really care for the P word.

Viv frowned. "I mean, I love you?"

Ness nodded. "Yep. Anyway, I've got plans. So, I better go."

Viv quirked an eyebrow. "Plans?"

"Video games."

"Gotcha."

"Talk to you later." Ness ended the Wisper session.

Ness did not have video game plans. She didn't have any kind of plans. She stepped away from the computer.

She wasn't paranoid or anxious or crazy. Those words were inadequate clumsy Plato's allegory of the cave shadows of what she actually was, and she hated that no understood it.

She just needed to relax, right? Go out on the back deck maybe. That easy. Yoga breathing. Fuck them.

Ness went to the back door. She stared at the doorknob. Her arms worked. Her hand worked. She could open the door. She could go out there. But just imagining it, just picturing herself stepping out onto the back deck strangled her lungs and her heart and her head and she couldn't breathe and she wanted to scream and she felt weak and pathetic and angry and sad and broken.

She didn't go outside. She went to the kitchen. She sat down on the linoleum with the lights off and she cried for an hour.

"Grams!" Ness waved at the camera when her grandmother's image rendered on Wisper.

Grams's response was more muted. She nodded. "Hi," she said. Grams had dark purple hair styled into funky old lady spikes. Give her some chunky bracelets and a choker and she'd be the spitting image of Ness from 1996. It gave Ness hope that time was ultimately more of a loop than a straight line.

Ness ate an onion-flavored crunch snack. "What's new with my favorite octogenarian?"

"Nothing really."

"Nothing?" Ness repeated, not bothering to hide her disappointment. "I count on you for hot goss, Grams. You're holding out on me. What's shaking with that UPS guy and his tight shorts?"

"You know you don't have to check on me all the time," Grams said. "I've been on my own for a while, Vanessa."

"Whu?" Ness managed through a mouth full. She hadn't checked in with Grams in over a week.

"I know you're lonely with Vivian working all the time, but I have things to do. I can't chat with you all day."

Ness wasn't sure if she was losing her mind or if Grams was. "What are you talking about?"

"Twice in the same day is too many times," Grams said. "The UPS guy only comes once."

Gabe shot a mini herd of zombies before they could eat Ness's brains. "Hey!"

"Huh?"

"What are you doing?"

Ness had Wisper video turned off. She said it was so they could focus on the video game, but the truth was, she was sleuthing. "Making fat stacks to pay your way over market-rate salary," she answered.

"Yeah, I googled you, boss. I don't think you need any more stacks." Gabe reloaded his shotgun.

Ness had a half dozen screens of server logs open, but she took a moment to switch out to a flamethrower. "You shouldn't google your boss."

"When your boss is a weird drone rich lady, you should absolutely google her."

"Okay, well you shouldn't tell your boss that you googled her." There. Ness found the traffic she was looking for. "And also, everyone always needs more fat stacks. America. Wall Street. Michael Douglas. Greed is good etcetera."

"Alright, oligarch. Do you wanna do this later then so you can have a computer hacker montage?"

"No," Ness told him. "Just a sec."

Gabe paused their game. "Did you really make Mark Zuckerberg cry?"

"Of course not. Probably not."

"Weird answer, boss. What about Bitcoin. Did you invent that?"

Ness shook her head. "Don't believe everything you google." She stared at her screen. "That isn't possible."

"I'm pretty sure Bitcoin is possible. I know a guy. He has one and he's going buy one of those ghost cities in Italy now."

"No." Ness shook her head again and took her hands off the keyboard for a little flail. "What the fuck?"

"Do you want to talk to me like a conversation or do you want to just say things?"

"Someone called my grandmother," Ness said. "With Wisper."

"Who?"

"Me."

". . . uh huh?"

"But it wasn't me."

"Is this a koan?"

"Must be a hacker. Using my account somehow . . . and my IP address? And a video filter so that Grams thought it was me?"

"Did you drunk dial your grandma and forget about it maybe?"

Ness shook her head. "I did not." No fucking hacker could out hack her. She hacked the planet before breakfast. She had stickers. She chased the traffic back. Whoever it was, calling Grams and stealing hot UPS guy gossip, well, Ness wasn't going to let that slide.

"I don't think anyone could log into your account that isn't you," Gabe said. "Your security is . . ."

"Don't say paranoid," Ness warned.

"I was going to say thorough as fuck. It took me like two

hours to do that setup assessment. It's like a dating profile fucked a job interview."

Ness's specialty was software that thought like a person. Her security was designed to emulate that scene in the movie where you ask questions to make sure your best friend hadn't been replaced by an alien body snatcher. The profile setup insured that at every login the user would be prompted with an all-new question that it would be impossible for anyone else to answer.

"In two years my security is going to run the world," Ness said.

"Yeah? Who called your grandma then?"

Ness flipped off her monitor and bared her teeth at it like a ferocious wolf mother protecting her cubs.

Viv wasn't answering. It was the middle of her super science time so Ness wasn't surprised, but also she was irritable about it and not feeling patient.

The Wisper call to Grams came from the lab, from Ness's workstation. But Ness hadn't been to the lab in months. It got more complicated. Ness remoted into the lab network and reviewed the logs on her workstation. The last login to it was her login and the local Wisper logs didn't show the call to Grams. Which meant someone either spoofed the IP address—which shouldn't be possible—or edited the logs on the Wisper server, which also shouldn't be possible. All of which didn't explain the biggest question of all: why? What possible reason would someone have to go through so much trouble just to have a seven-minute conversation with a purple haired 82-year-old about the UPS guy's butt?

Maybe Ness did need a computer hacker montage.

She paced around her house, anxious and anxiouser with every step. She was a Very Logical smart person and the most logical explanation was that there was no super cyberpunk hacker but that she had lost her damn mind. How far of a trip was that really? She already had a half dozen diagnoses from the DSM-5 and a bathroom cabinet full of mood stabilizers, antidepressants, anti-anxiety cocktails, and cherry flavored antacids. Maybe this was it? Four months of quarantine was all the nudge necessary to push her from a marginally functional agoraphobic with obsessive compulsive tics to a full-on psychotic break.

"Shit," she said. "Shitshitshitshit." She glared at her screen and sat back down in front of it. If Viv wasn't going answer maybe someone else would. She started a Wisper call to herself.

"Hey buddy, that doesn't work. You can't call yourself silly," Wisper told her, because of course she'd given it a sassy attitude.

"Fucker."

Then she had another idea. Even she couldn't answer Grams's custom security question but that didn't matter. She was the Wisper Master, a digital god with divine power over her domain. Let there be administrative privileges, she decreed, and there was and it was good. She bypassed the security and just like that she was pretending to be an old lady.

"Moment of truth," she said and started the call. It was answered almost immediately which was the least unexpected part.

"Dude!" Ness said to Ness and waved. "It's you."

Ness didn't just look like Ness, which some kind of deep fake filter might have been able to pull off, but Ness was also apparently sitting in Ness's living room and wearing Ness's hoody.

Ness nodded at her doppelgänger and then disconnected from the Wisper call.

So that was that. She had lost her damn mind.

A call came in from Wisper. Ness.

"Fuck." Did her psychotic break have a Wisper account now?

Ness clicked the thing and locked eyes with herself again.

"Don't hang up," Other Ness said. "You're not losing it. I can explain." Other Ness smiled. "It's really cool."

"Just keep your video off at first, okay?" Ness said.

"Got it," Other Ness said. "This is gonna be awesome."

"Straight face. Straight face."

"You're talking to yourself."

"Well, yeah."

Gabe connected to the Wisper call. "You don't look like my grandmother, boss."

Ness blinked, remembering she was still using Grams's account. "I have to show you something."

Gabe shrugged. "Alright."

"Ta-dah!" Other Ness said, revealing herself.

Gabe was quiet for a moment. "So you're super bored, huh?"

"This isn't a trick," Ness told. "That's me. I'm me. We're both me."

"Me in stereo," Other Ness said.

"See, she's the me from a parallel universe. Viv was right! But she was totally wrong. The static isn't Jupiter's little brother. It's infinite parallel universes. I used a lot of the same code base for Viv's Teletubby microphone and Wisper and the wires got all crossed, I guess. I'm still—we're still—debugging it. But she called Grams and didn't get her Grams. She got my Grams."

"I see," Gabe's face was emotionless, placid. A nice day in the park. Plain yogurt face.

Ness wished she could be explaining this all to Viv, but she still wasn't answering. Gabe was going to have to do, but he needed to be more excited.

"This is fucking awesome," Other Ness said.

"But like there are—"

"—so many implications." The Nesses finished each other's sentences.

"Turns out our worlds are almost identical," Ness continued. "It's not like her world has flesh eating spider people or Matthew McConaughey is president or anything."

"Same Tangerine fuckface." Other Ness frowned.

"But we are wearing different socks today." Ness held up a socked foot to the camera. Other Ness did the same.

Gabe nodded. "Uh huh."

"And it's seven hours later over there."

Other Ness nodded. "I think there's some temporal displacement, like how light bends in a funhouse mirror, you know?"

"Sure," Gabe told them.

"How familiar are you with quantum theory?" Ness asked him.

"Hold on." Gabe grabbed something from off camera. A loaded vaporizer. He took a long, deep hit.

"Are you getting high right now?" Other Ness asked him.

"Yeah. How are you not?"

"Shit, should we conference in your Gabe?" Ness asked Other Ness. "You have a Gabe right? I didn't ask you that before."

"I've got a Gabe," Other Ness said. "I think he's got a different haircut though."

"Don't conference in any other Gabes," Gabe pleaded. "Not until I'm way, way more stoned."

"Was Professor Lashley handsy on your side too?" Other Ness asked Ness.

Ness's eyes widened. "So handsy."

"Creepo."

Gabe let out a soft whine that turned into an anguished cry. "What the shit is happening?" He slapped his face and shook his head.

"Wait," Other Ness said. She grabbed her monitor for emphasis. "We could shoot some zombie motherfuckers."

Ness flashed devil horns. "Yesssssss."

Gabe vaporized himself out of consciousness within an hour. His head fell forward, headset still on, controller in hand, high resolution video streaming.

"How are you?" Other Ness asked.

Ness took a sip from a can of Dr. Pepper. "Pretty good."

"No. For real. How are you doing?"

Ness almost cried. "It's hard, right?"

"Yeah."

"Just . . ."

"Everything."

"Yeah." Ness pulled at her short hair. "Can you . . ?" How could she not even talk to herself about this? "How's the fresh air on your side?"

"Probably the same as it is on yours," Other Ness said. The look in her eyes was enough to make it clear that they were as alike as their worlds.

"Viv doesn't really get it."

"My Viv doesn't either. I mean, she's awesome."

"Right. The best."

"But . . ."

"It's hard."

"Yep."

"Fuuuuuck." Ness leaned back into her couch. "What's wrong with us?"

Other Ness looked off, away from the camera. "COVID makes it so much worse, yeah? I went to the window this morning and I . . . it's like I could see it out there. Swirling around like smoke."

Even with all the windows and doors sealed tight, Ness scrubbed her skin pink in the shower five times a day. "They don't have better pills over there, huh?"

Other Ness chewed her thumb, shook her head.

"Is this like next level narcissism or something? We can only relate to ourselves."

Other Ness shrugged. "I think we're pretty charming."

"Same."

"What would Dr. Prithi think?"

"Oh, you still see Prithi?"

"You don't?"

"She got pregnant here!"

Other Ness grinned. "Good for her!"

"I bet we could tell each other things. Stuff we can't say to ourselves."

"I bet we could," Other Ness agreed.

Neither of them said anything.

Gabe snored audibly.

"I think we broke him," Ness said.

Other Ness nodded. "Probably."

"I like you," Ness said. She wasn't flirting with herself, or at least she didn't think she was flirting with herself. Would that just be masturbation? It sounded so dumb, so self-serving, so what-the-actual-fuck-is-wrong-with-you-crazy-Vanessa? Do you really have such low esteem that you need to tell yourself you're not a sack of broken glass?

"Same," Other Ness said and then shook her head. Her eyes got wet. "I like you too."

"I should probably . . ." Ness trailed off.

Other Ness nodded. "Me too."

"Is this going to work again tomorrow?" Ness was afraid the answer would be no.

"I'm pretty sure it will," Other Ness said. "We'll find out either way."

"Yeah."

"So. Later?"

"Later."

Ness closed out of Wisper. She gathered her knees up on the couch. She cried but it was a good cry. It wasn't a grown-up disaster desperate anxiety cry. It was an I like me cry and it was the best cry she'd had since the world started to end.

Ness fell asleep on the couch and woke up to a Wisper call that said it was Grams. But was it really Grams? Ness checked the time. Past eleven in the morning. Ness set Wisper to accept voice commands so she could start making coffee.

"Accept," she said and started filling coffee thing with filtered water. Grams's face rendered, looking serious. "What's up, rockstar?"

Grams twisted her lips around, thinking though what she was going to say. "You said . . . well. You said . . . that you need to call you. It was important."

Ness froze. "Shit. Are you okay?"

"I'd like you to explain all of this to me but . . ." A mischievous glint came to her eye. "UPS delivery day." She winked.

"Good for you, Grams. I'll call you later. I'll try to explain. 'kay?"

"Okay."

Ness realized she'd timed out of Grams's account while she was sleeping and Wisper still wouldn't let Ness call Ness. She took three minutes to put an exception for that in the server-side code and called herself. Other Ness answered and she looked upset.

"What's going on?"

"Viv," Other Ness said. "Tell me she called you back?"

Ness checked her Wisper log to confirm. "Nope. Must have pulled an all-nighter."

Other Ness shook her head. Tears rolled down her cheeks. "It wasn't an all-nighter, Ness."

"Oh fuck."

It wasn't COVID. The whole world was in lockdown panic and Viv was going to die from something that had been diagnosed when she was seven years old. Too many skipped meals. Too much insulin. The kind of thing that could always almost happen and this time it did.

"Gabe!" Ness shouted when he answered her call.

"Ness!" he shouted right back her. His tone and facial expression changed immediately when he got a full sense of her face, tear-streaked, shaking. "What's going on?"

"You have to come over."

Gabe nodded. "Yep. I need twelve minutes."

"Don't hang up. Turn the video off if you need to, I can't . . ." Ness heart was going off like a machine gun. She gulped at air like a goldfish flopping around on the rug. "I need you to stay on with me, okay?"

"Deal," Gabe said. He turned the video off and she could hear him running to his car. "Do you want to talk or . . ?"

"Just say things!"

"Did you listen to that podcast I told you about?"

"No," Ness shook her head. He talked about so many podcasts. "Tell me about it again. Just keep talking. Please."

Other Ness couldn't stay on the line. She fell apart just like Ness was falling apart. They were two anvil people thrashing around on a frozen-over pond. It wasn't helpful for them to be close together right now. Ness was always Ness's worst enemy.

Ness didn't register most of what Gabe was saying, but it did help to hear his voice. He was a tiny thin thread she could hold onto. She went into all of her closets, tore through them. She muted herself and screamed and kicked the wall.

"I'm pulling up to your gate," Gabe said. He was wrong. It didn't take him twelve minutes. Gabe made the drive in nine.

"I'm coming!"

"You're . . ?"

"Yeah." Ness stood at her front door. "I think."

"Open the gates, boss. I'll—"

Ness shook her head. "No, I can't. The security doesn't . . . There's facial recognition built in. If it's not me, or Viv, the gate won't open."

"That's . . ."

"Paranoid," Ness agreed. It was also code that would take way too longer to bypass even if she could manage to focus enough to do it.

She took the deepest breath she'd ever taken in her life and opened the door. She ran as fast as she could as if she could outrun the chemicals that made her brain work the way it did. She made it five steps and fell down on her knees, her whole body shaking, her head spinning.

"Boss!"

She was going to pass out.

Wisper dinged. Someone calling into the conference.

"Accept," Ness stuttered.

"You are so fucking awesome," Other Ness said. "You're strong. Stronger than a minotaur."

". . . a minotaur?" Gabe was all minotaur judgemental from the other side of the security gate, close enough she could see the diseases crawling all over his exposed skin.

"Minotaurs are rad, Gabe," Ness said.

"Yeah, shut up, Gabe."

". . . sorry."

"Come on, Nessie. You can do this."

Ness wanted to do it. She wanted to just be okay, go outside, save the girl. Easy. But she'd been telling herself the same thing for forever and it didn't matter. It wasn't like pushing a few extra reps on the weight machine. She couldn't try herself healthy.

"I . . . can't."

"New plan," Other Ness said. The gate let out a loud beep and opened.

"Oh shit!" Gabe ran through the gate.

"What the fuck?" Ness managed. That shouldn't be possible.

"I hacked the neighborhood power grid," Other Ness said. "Maybe killed electric for like a hundred houses. Very illegal."

Gabe helped Ness sit up. "Are you sick? Do you need a hospital? Funyons? Talk to me, boss."

"Not me," Ness said.

"It's Viv," Other Ness said. "I can't hack security at the lab."

Ness grimaced. "Redundant offline power generators." Because of earthquakes and meteor strikes and giant super diseases and . . . paranoia.

"Exposition please, boss. I'm freaking out."

"Get me to your car," Ness said.

Gabe pulled her off the ground.

"I'm going to scream a lot and I might pee," Ness warned.

"Jesus, boss."

She did scream and her vision blurred and she bit her lip until it bled. But she didn't pee. A full-on Godzilla panic attack. It ended—sort of—when she was in Gabe's car. Other Ness gave Gabe the address to the lab.

"Break laws," Other Ness advised.

"Sure thing, boss." He looked over at Ness—his Ness. "Or second boss." He blinked and took in the details of Ness's outfit. "Skiing jacket?"

Ness was wearing five layers from her toes to the top of her head. She had a mask and two scarves wrapped around her mouth. She had hats and a hood. "I can't explain this right now." She'd have to make that her next tattoo.

Gabe grabbed her multiple-gloved hand. "Don't have to," he said.

Other Ness told Gabe some of the details about Viv while they drove, and Ness tried to get her shit under control.

"And you can't just call an ambulance because . . ?"

"Facial recognition," Ness chimed in. Security. Ness's fortune and almost certainly some kind of municipal law violation.

"Vanessa," Ness said. "I need you to tell me."

"Don't," Other Ness said.

"Your . . ."

"Please, don't."

"What happened over there?"

Other Ness was quiet a moment. "I made it out the door like you did. But my Gabe couldn't get to me. The fire department went to the lab but it's like Fort Knox. It took them too long." Ness could hear Other Ness crying. "My Viv might be okay. But . . . she might not be."

"Got it," Ness said. Somehow all that awful hit her right in the Get Shit Done part of her brain and the anxiety fog cleared just a little bit. "Gabe, no matter what happens, no matter what I say, you drag my ass in front of the door to the lab. You use me like a fucking skeleton key to get in there and get to Viv."

Gabe nodded, resolute. "I can do that." He drove through a red. "She's going to be okay, boss." Cars screamed past, blurs sounding horns. "Both of them are. I know it."

They skidded to a stop in front of the lab.

"Let's go!" Gabe got out of the car like an action hero, leaving the door open to run around to Ness's side.

"Maybe this time, you can, Ness," Other Ness said.

Ness clenched her fists. She didn't believe in fairy tales or in herself. She was a pretty shitty liar.

Gabe dragged Ness out of the car.

"You need to take the things off . . . my face," Ness squeezed through staccato breathes.

Gabe pulled off her hats and scarves. The sun was so bright it burned through her. Solar radiation. Tumors and malaria probably.

Wisper dinged. Another caller. And then another. And then another.

"Accept all," Ness mumbled.

"Dude," Another Ness said. "You kick a million asses."

"I'm scared, too, but we can do this together," Fourth Ness said.

And then there were too many of them, overlapping, coming from so many worlds.

"I love you," one said.

"There's nothing wrong with you, Ness. You're not broken."

"Where did you get that t-shirt? That's sick!"

Ness laughed. She wept like a dam burst inside her skull. Waterfall face. She felt her feet on the parking lot hard top. She felt Gabe keeping her steady. She picked up her chin just a little.

"Ladies, we're fucking unstoppable," she said.

And the door to the lab opened with a ka-chunk.

mMeEsDslaUgMe

Mark Teppo

"Your subliminals have been hacked," Petra announced to the room of pasty-white Burliedge executives. The overhead lights in the twentieth-floor boardroom had been dimmed, and through the polarizing of her glasses, the faces of the executives were like a sea of full moons. Reflecting the stark display of the ad projected onto the screen at the front of the room.

Burliedge's fall clothing line, on full display—at twice life-size. A pair of airbrushed models hugged each other, with nothing but pure emptiness filling the void behind them. The pair were wearing two of the company's new overcoats: the one on the left was covered in optical patterns that blurred and warped, even when reduced to the flat two-dimensionality of the screen; the one on the right was covered with spectrum-shifted geometric shapes—blues bleeding into greens, yellows slipping toward black. The two women wore frozen expressions of distant and oblique sensuality. You were supposed to want to be them without actually wanting them. It was a fine distinction in advertising: creating an illusion of desirability without descending into awkward intimations of lesbian lust.

That much the creative team had gotten right. Marketing expected stellar results from the ad campaign, but a vice president's wife had started crying when she had casually seen the proofs on her husband's desk. She hadn't been able to articulate why the image affected her so, but the vice president had been in advertising long enough to know that something was wrong with the image's subliminal messaging.

Burliedge's chief executive called in an expert.

Petra approached the glowing screen with some reluctance. Even with her glasses dialed to the maximum, the hidden geometries of the designs made her eyes water. "Here," she said, sketching in the empty plane in front of the screen with her light pen. "In the white spaces you don't think to look at because you think they're empty. There's an echo of a text message. It's clever, but it's the first place any good sublimist will strain content." She drew hashmarks across the coat of the righthand model, blocking out the dopplered triangles on the coat. "Down here, though, is the real trick."

She closed one eye as she sketched. The geometries were fighting her efforts to obscure them, trying to crawl around the hashmarks. Trying to influence her to draw their outline instead of the image she was sublimating. She was an old pro, though, and could withstand the sight of the yawning Abyss, but to stand long on that precipice drained one's spirit.

Someone behind her gasped, which was all the indication she needed to know she was done. She clicked off her pen as she turned away from the screen.

With the screen behind her, all the moon faces were in extra relief. Distorted and haggard. She saw shock and horror and even—yes, over there in the corner; there's one in every crowd, isn't there?—arousal.

The line of text she had indicated wavered and danced, its letters spelling out an explicitly gleeful celebration of necrophilia. The image she had revealed showed that the models were rotting corpses beneath the coats. The woman in front—the one who seemed a touch more aroused and eager than the other—was being devoured by a pair of hyenas. Their muzzles were buried between her legs, chewing and gnawing.

"You have a leak," Petra said to the chief executive who had requested her analysis of the image as she returned to the far end of the boardroom table.

Burliedge's CEO looked at her, his face torn with disgust and embarrassment. "Who did this?" he asked in a strangled voice.

"That degree of sublimation requires access to the source files," she said as she slipped her jacket on.

It had been designed to her rather specific instructions. It was similar in style to Burliedge's new fall overcoat, but hers had been designed to very specific instructions that were more about security and integrity than fashion and subliminal messaging. A shiver ran up her spine as the comfortable security of the jacket wrapped itself around her frame.

"You'll be inclined to think it is one of your art techs with a grudge," she continued, "but they can be influenced. They could be given instructions as to how to imbed both the text and the image, and have no recollection of doing the work. A good sublimist works by proxy. They'd never expose themselves directly. In my opinion, one of your competitors hired a sublimist, but I doubt you'll ever find a money trail."

"Can this be salvaged?" the CEO asked.

"No," she said. "You'll have to black out most of what you want consumers to look at."

"And why wouldn't we do just that?" he asked.

It sounded like a rhetorical question, but she answered it nonetheless. Just to make sure her message was understood.

"Burliedge's position in the marketplace is one that is bolstered by tradition and elegance," she said as she adjusted the scarf around her neck. "You don't do cheap marketing gimmicks where you tease your customers like this. These coats are a revision of an already successful design. You aren't iterating enough to warrant such coquettishness. Your customers will, ultimately, be disappointed if you approach them in this fashion."

"We've already paid for the placements," one of the other executives said. "We can't back out."

Petra glanced at the man on the other side of the table who hadn't flinched away from the image she had suggested on the screen. He was staring intently at her as she reached under the collar of her jacket for the white earbuds that filtered out most of the audible frequencies.

"Necrophilia or nothingness," she said. "Ask yourself which you want for your customers . . ."

A cab waited for her under the chrome and neon awning that sheltered the front entrance of Burliedge's forty-floor world headquarters. Beyond, the night was dappled with glittering rain. A security guard held the car door for her, and she inclined her head in gratitude as she slid into the car.

"Where to?" the cabbie asked. He was a thin man with sallow features, a grey-flecked beard, and a woolen cap.

"Midtown," she said. She didn't offer anything more specific, and the cabbie shrugged as if it didn't matter all that much to him either as long as she paid the fare.

She leaned back against the hard seat, listening to the random patter of the rain against the roof of the cab. Whatever mysteries there were out in the natural world, they communicated in a way that was still well beyond human comprehension. Thankfully. The not-quite-as-mysterious was problematic enough.

Burliedge's latest designs had been influenced—that much was true—but the subliminals weren't the work of any submits that she knew. The geometries suggested by the patterns were of . . . foreign origin. Human brains didn't operate like that, not without assistance.

Petra's phone vibrated in the breast pocket of her coat. She slipped it out and pressed the two tattooed fingers of her right hand against the glass surface. The phone recognized her, and turned its screen on.

How was your meeting? A text read. It was from Ambrose, the youngest of their coterie.

She pulled the collar of her jacket open and slipped her tattooed fingertips underneath her scarf. She found the ridged tissue at the hollow of her throat—the silver-laced brand of the five-branched tree—and the metal reacted to the ink in her fingers. "A satisfactory conclusion," she whispered, and the words appeared on the screen of her phone.

Shall we spread rumors?

She thought of the man who had been watching her at the end of the meeting. The gleam in his eyes. The hunger, hiding within his pudgy frame.

"No," she whispered. "We should remain obtuse. Invisible."

Her phone remained dark for a long time, long enough that she began to worry, but then another message came through.

You need to tell X.

"I know," she said. "I am going to see him now."

An animated image appeared on the screen. A fat rodent of some indeterminate species, shoving an entire donut in its mouth, over and over again. Petra smiled, and tapped the image away with her fingers. She felt the influence of the subliminal in the image sweep into her mind. Fat. Content. Happy.

Ambrose could always read her mood, even when he wasn't in the same room. He wouldn't push her to talk, but he knew when something was on her mind. The fat rodent was his way of saying that he understood, and would wait patiently for her to tell him.

He was an eternally optimistic fool. Such a rare trait in any person, much less a sublimist.

She slouched down farther in the back seat of the cab, reaching for her earbuds. She slipped them into her ears, and the sound of the cab became a distant groan. The rain against the roof vanished entirely. She tapped up her music library on her phone and flicked through until she found Beethoven. *The Sixth Symphony.* On a good night, the ride would talk less than fifteen minutes—enough time for the first movement. On a bad night, she might hear the whole symphony.

Hope spring eternal, she thought, mindful of the influence of Ambrose's animated image. The lush sound of stringed instruments filled her head, and she let her mind drift— present but absent from any sensory input. Safe from outside influences.

She caught a second cab in Midtown, and had it drive her counter-clockwise around Central Park. It dropped her off two blocks south of where the first cab had deposited her, and she walked another block south before ducking into an alley marked with distressed paint that glowed in her glasses.

She walked seventy and seven paces, and then stopped beside a dented dumpster also marked with glowing paint. Behind it, spray painted on the wall, was a distorted face. She traced her tattooed fingers along its features: corner of mouth to opposite corner, nostril to nostril, up the bridge to the eyes, and then up to the third eye in the center of the forehead. It was a pattern that would appear comical to an outsider, but she had traced a line similar to the scar of branches and trunk at the base of her throat.

Behind her, the lock in an unmarked door opened with a loud clunk. She touched her fingertips to her lips and then placed them against the lintel of the door as she slipped inside the dark building. The door swung shut behind her, the lock engaging automatically, and she stood silently in the darkness. Waiting for the thermal and UV scans to finish. She knew they were done when a weak line of lights stuttered to life in the floor. She followed it to a narrow staircase that took her several flights down into one of the more remote basements of the Museum of Modern Art.

Where the Chapel of Vigilant Recursion was located.

The door was old growth timber layered over a steel core, and the threshold was sealed with a hundred and twenty tiles marked with the sanctuary sigil. Inside, the room was octagonal, and a large multiform panel painted in the Rothko style hung on each wall. The center of the room was sunk several meters below the floor, and its own walls were lined with cabinets and bookcases. There was a table and eight chairs in the center of the sunken center, and seated at the table was a man several years older than Petra.

X. The alphabetical eldest of the subversive sublimists. In person, he answered to Xavier, much in the same way she answered to Petra. And like Ambrose, cherry-cheeked neophyte, new to their ranks.

Xavier's jacket—made by the same tailor as hers, but in a subterranean-soiled brown to her night-tinged burgundy—hung on the back of his chair. He wore a grey t-shirt and equally unobtrusive slacks, and perched on his nose were a pair of unassuming reading spectacles. A stubble of white hair crowned his head, and his skin was pale and waxy in the Chapel's light. He had been reading a book, and he put it down when Petra entered the room.

There was a bottle of wine on the table and two glasses, one half-full. He poured the red wine into the second glass as Petra navigated the short stairs down to the communion core of the chapel. She undid the snaps and straps of her jacket, but stopped short of removing it entirely. She pulled her scarf off and dropped it on the table as Xavier offered her the glass of wine.

She took the glass with a nod, and tilted it so that she could dip her two tattooed fingers in the dark wine. A red rivulet ran down her fingers as she touched her throat and then her lips. She flicked what remained onto the wooden floor of the communion core, and held her fingers out to Xavier, who repeated the same sequence with his own wine.

"Eyes to the stars," she said as their wine-darkened fingertips touched.

"Ears to the ground," he replied.

"Heart to the sea," they both said, and then drank from their glasses.

The wine was a Moncerbal from Bierzo, in Spain. It had been bottled at least a decade ago and it had aged well.

"What are you reading?" she asked, putting the wine glass down on the table and resuming the removal of her jacket. It wasn't the question foremost in her mind when she looked at his sunken cheeks and dark eyes, but she could guess the answer to that question.

"Philosophical Italian poetry," he said, showing her the cover of the book. "Written by a disgruntled idealist, who dreams of a world filled with sentient Neo-Futurist and Brutalist buildings. They copulate and make tiny buildings."

"Charming," Petra offered.

Xavier lifted his shoulders slightly. "It sounds worse than it is. The writer has some talent rhyme that I wish he would embrace more wholeheartedly. As it is, I sense he loathes himself a little more every time he suffers a couplet to survive."

Petra kicked out the chair from the table and flopped into it. She gulped at her wine, wishing she wasn't but glad to feel the cool liquid gliding down her throat.

"That bad?" Xavier asked.

She lifted her shoulders and took another swallow of wine. "It's done. Burliedge will cancel the campaign. They'll spend months chasing ghosts in their art pipeline. And their designer will second-guess himself next time. We have stifled their efforts this time, but . . ."

"Ah, I knew there had to be a catch," Xavier sighed.

"One of the middle managers was paying too much attention to me," she said. "I don't know if he has odd kinks or if he wasn't influenced by my pen. If it is the latter and he can get the right person's attention, this could all come undone."

"Our influence is diffuse," Xavier said. "Even if they do suspect malfeasance, they can't track it. And there is always someone who looks away at the wrong time. But they're just one set of eyeballs. One voice. They can't shift corporate paranoia."

"I know," she sighed. Xavier was right. They—she—had managed to influence an entire corporation and not leave any trace of their subliminal activities. It had started with a year ago, when she had met the vice president's wife at a society party out in the Hamptons. During a brief interlude in the lady's room, she had implanted a subliminal hook in the other woman—a tiny hook she could hang a psychological reaction to whenever she needed to. And when Burliedge had first announced the new patterns for the fall line, she had arranged to run into the vice president's wife at a charity fundraiser. She had implanted a psychosomatic reaction in the wife, one that would be triggered at the sight of binary optical illusions. An overwhelming sense of guilt and shame, followed by bouts of vomiting and self-flagellation. The VP had assumed the ad itself had been hacked, and Burliedge had called in a specialist.

But what she had told them was hidden in the image was what she had drawn with the light pen. Not that they would ever realize they had been influenced in real-time; she had coded an aversion to thinking about such subterfuge into the necrophilia messaging. Layers upon layers. The message and the medium had become interchangeable.

It had been risky work, and one that had split the coterie of Chapelists divisively when they had argued for doing it. In the end, she and Xavier were granted the anonymity to do what needed to be done, but none of the others could ever know. Some influences were self-generative, and it was safer for all of them to remain unaware.

But it had to be done. The eldritch influencers were getting bolder. Seeking to move into the mainstream. Forcing themselves upon the rest of humanity. Trying to leverage the darkness that lurked deep in the murky muck of the mind—that instinctive lizard brain terror of knowing the futility and pointlessness of existence.

"We should tell Darien at EFT," Xavier said.

Eight-Fold Textures were an upstart clothing manufacturer that had offices across the river in Hoboken, New Jersey, in a converted meat packing plant. Darien Ruttleage—their CEO—was a speed-talking millennial with degrees in

Acting and Marketing from NYU. He liked to trash talk the rotting centenarians of the fashion industry, and among the Chapelists, there was an on-going argument whether he had a sublimist on his payroll or an inordinately natural talent at public speaking. He was also a brilliant strategist at anticipating and reacting to shifts in the markets, and fore-knowledge of Burliedge's lack of advertising presence for the fall would be very welcome insight.

"If we do, he won't be subtle enough," Petra said. "Burliedge will jump to the conclusion that EFT is behind the hack, and none of their reactions will be good."

The worst case scenario was that Burliedge would publish the images anyway and ship the clothes without alterations. Neither the necrophiliac messaging nor the images of wild hyaenas chewing their way through young bellies were actually there. The clothes would sell—rapidly, in fact, spurred on by the marketing-driven rumor that there was something amiss in the fabrics. In the fall, the streets would be filled with people wearing the equivalent of sandwich boards. All with the same message—the one the Chapelists hoped to suppress. *Kill yourself for the Dead God; do it now for He is Coming and He is Hungry.*

The oldest marketing manual in existence—the first and foremost of the subliminal ur-texts—stated, in a moment of frank clarity, that there were giants in the earth in those days, and to worship these giants was to worship nihilism and fatalism. The giants had been drowned, but their ethos was survived, spinning on down the centuries until it had become something so foreign and alien as to be indecipherable. But that didn't mean it wasn't apprehensible. Would enough misery and degradation within the human species bring these forgotten monsters back? None of the Chapelists knew for certain, but they were all united in a desire to never find out. Perhaps their efforts were merely an attempt to counter the bleak finality of that cold, drowned truth. A futile fabrication, equally hand-crafted as the old marketing manual, but one they could call themselves the architects of, and in doing so, give themselves meaning.

The need to communicate was the primal difference between man and beast, after all. Unfortunately, it came with a desire to not be alone, and the universe was a very big place that cared so very little for these bi-pedal hominids who fancied themselves dreamers and creators.

Xavier finished his wine, and put the empty glass on the table. "We are too frightened of being found out," he said.

"And what is the alternative?" Petra asked. They had had conversations like this many times before, and while Petra didn't disagree with the sentiment of Xavier's statement, she (and some of the others) were concerned about the arrogance that would grow in the absence of caution.

"It's all speculative," Xavier said.

"All existence is speculation," Petra countered. "Except in the case of corporate entities. We know what they will do when threatened."

"And so we do nothing." Xavier pulled his lips down.

Petra glared at him over the rim of her glass. "That is an unkind assessment of what we accomplished today," she said.

"But what about tomorrow?" he asked. "Or next season?"

"I think you've been reading too much philosophical Italian poetry."

Xavier sniffed, and pushed the book he had been reading with a knuckle. "This one will be a problem if he ever finds an audience," he said.

"And so we'll deal with him before he gets that far," Petra said. "If he gets that far. Didn't you say that he has a flair for couplets? I would see that a sign that he hasn't fully succumbed to ennui. There may still be hope."

Xavier looked at her, his eyes hooded and inscrutable. The Chapelists were a continuum, from the eager innocence of Ambrose to the Xavier's sullen fatalism, and each played a vital role in maintaining the equilibrium of their anonymity. But there were too many weary elders now—even with the recent deaths of Zachariah and Yolande—and the balance was teetering. Some of the younger sublimists saw opportunities in the missing letters of their organization, and were in a rush to acquire position without the requisite scarring and hardening that would armor them against external influences.

A sublimist's message was only effective when an audience was unaware they were being influenced. Should the Chapel be illuminated, their ability to influence would be severely diminished. Unlike the eldritch influencers, who had burrowed so deep into the degenerate leavings of past generations that short of a God walking the streets of New York or London or Buenos Aries, they could never be revealed.

And yet, these ancient influencers wanted exactly that: a God on the streets. *He is Coming and He is Hungry.*

"Perhaps," Xavier said. He picked up the book of poetry as

he stood. "You did good work today, Petra," he said.

"Thank you," she said, dipping her head.

He laid a hand on her shoulder and gave a reassuring squeeze. "Perhaps . . ." he started.

He didn't finish and Petra put her hand over his. "Perhaps," she said too, suggesting that she knew what he was going to say and that—perhaps—it wasn't necessary to say out loud. He gave her shoulder a final squeeze, and then put on his jacket and left the Chapel.

Perhaps, she thought after he was gone, none of us will be necessary tomorrow.

But she knew—just as he did—that would not be the case. And the thought weighed on her, much in the same way she knew it weighed on him.

She would meditate on the paintings hung on the walls, seeking solace in the subtle variations in the uniformity of the colors. But it would take many hours to refill her soul, and it was unlikely she could restore her spirit fully. She was too close to the end of the alphabet now. Highly effective and efficient with her manipulations, but so scarred. So inured to feeling anything.

Each time we exert our influence, we isolate ourselves a little more, she reflected. She leaned over and poured herself a full glass of wine. And there is no way to undo what we have done.

She took out her phone, and called up her message log. On the screen, the fat rodent ate and ate and ate its donut. Eternally happy to be trapped in its loop. She watched it, a faint smile tugging at her mouth.

Perhaps, she thought, choosing one of the possible futures still unstained. *Perhaps, I will call him . . .*

Turn Your Screen On

Kate Ristau

This is not a love story.

You always thought it was, but you're not here to write the ending, so it's mine now. And I never went for that romantic shit.

It's not your fault.

That's what I'm supposed to say, right? That you did what you could. You lived a good life. We will remember you fondly. Rest in Peace.

I'll end the meeting soon.

Gerard said you could beat *GoldenEye* with only one bullet. I don't believe him, but that doesn't mean I'm not trying.

I waited for you to log back on. Longer than I should have, really, but what else was there to do?

The computer told me I should shut down all extraneous applications and reduce oxygen intake to extend the life stuff.

Fuck the life stuff. What's the point anyway?

I'll keep losing at *GoldenEye*. Put Smash Mouth on a loop. Part of me finds it endlessly ironic to end my life replaying the moments it began. With music. With video games. With you. Without you.

I'm not being morbid. I'm singing All Star at the top of my lungs. Trying to remember the ending to *Face/Off*. Whose face was it anyway?

In training, Gerard told us about mental acuity—how to stay present and practicing. On the body. In the self. Aware and alive.

I've ignored all his advice. I'm an exercise in nostalgia. Six degrees of Kevin Bacon. Everything connects through *Tremors* or *Prince of Thieves*. Gerard's still dead, sitting in cold storage.

All storage is cold in space.

Your mom made us those DiGiorno pizzas. My mom never had that kind of money. How did we end up here? Luck, I guess. And so much Mountain Dew.

I should have grand and wonderful memories of you. I should speak of you like Kevin Costner with a bow and arrow. Grandiose. Grand. Granting. So people remember who you were. Ranting.

But I've stopped recording this meeting. No one's listening. You logged off.

I still hate you for that. I'm not supposed to. Big emotion. I didn't save the chat. I lost it for a bit there. I'll erase these files.

You locked yourself in. Barricaded the door. Deactivated the airlock with an emergency pickax. You didn't want me to get sick.

I tried. After you left. That's a euphemism. You didn't leave. You died. I licked all the keyboards. No one should see that.

We had those agar plates in high school, remember? They were supposed to show something about hand washing. Wipe the Q-tip on your dirty hand. Wash your hands. Wipe the Q-tip on your clean hand. Our results were inconclusive. The bacteria grew on the wrong side.

Mrs. Baldwin loved our project anyway. Of course she did. You were her golden boy.

Gerard thought we still had a chance. His dreams were always bigger than his science.

He didn't expect the space junk.

There's irony there, but I can't see it.

I'll log off soon.

The ship will crash land on A-0354. The fetuses are isolated. Raised by computers. Their bodies won't be timebombs. They'll watch old movies and listen to good music. Read literature. With a capital L.

They won't have Lucky Charms boxes. Social media. Kool-Aid.

You hated that manufactured world. Now, it's grounding me.

We lost too much pressure with the last hit. The O2 won't last.

The ship will detach Section Seven soon, jettison infected lifeforms.

If I keep talking about the ship, I won't have to talk about me. Or you.

Gerard says that's unhealthy. I told him we talk about that later. He laughed. Then he coughed. We stopped talking.

You shouldn't have left the meeting. No one should die alone out here. Not even you.

Space junk. That's what I called my butt. It made my sister laugh.

You hated her. She wanted you to. Made it easy. You both hated each other so much that you became best friends.

That's the thing I've learned. On the other side of all this.

The bad emotions are good. The Cheetos keep you sane. We live because we're dying.

I would take every dying moment with you over this extra time with an empty screen. I keep watching the waiting room.

You were selfish. I don't have to put that emotion away. Bottle it up. Not talk about it. Gerard likes it when we are fully Here. Well, he did. Before. Capital H. Feeling our feelings. He'd be proud of me. Not for the keyboard-licking. And he probably hates Smash Mouth. But for all the rest of it, he'd get that one smile that made him look a little oxygen-deprived. He'd like me Here. So, I'll settle into my seat. Feel my fingers, my hands, and say it again. You are selfish, and I am too. We live inside our own bubble until we let someone in.

I'd let you in again. But I wouldn't take this ending. I wouldn't write this goddamn story. Not without you.

I'd restart the whole level. Flip the power switch. Blow on the cartridge, then make some edits.

We should have logged off at the same time, but I couldn't push the button. Now all I have is soup. You ate the pizza, and Gerard is holed up with all that ice cream.

Did we deserve a new world? We messed up the other one.

Fuck that. Who cares?

We think too much.

It was John Travolta. He probably hoped we'd be singing *Grease*, in the end. His legacy. But we remember what we remember. And this last story is mine.

So, I'm playing *GoldenEye*. I'm eating soup. I'm singing Smash Mouth and I'm logging off. Not for you. For me. This is my story. And I'm not sharing it. Not anymore.

The only person I wanted to hear it was you.

I am going to erase those files. Rewrite. Let those kids imagine that we were better than we were. Noble. Righteous. Green Knight, and not *Con Air*.

We were more.

I'm going now. Popping the bubble.

I'll see you.

Costco

Jeb R. Sherril

"No," I said, gritting my teeth. "Never again. Never, ever, never, ever, ever, ever again."

"It's just a few things," Gary said, beaming his absurd smile at me as if that should somehow make me want to jump up and follow him straight into Hell.

"Just a few things?" I said, wanting very badly to leap from my warm bed and shout at my brother. What stopped me was the fact that I hadn't actually moved yet. Any one of a number of possible excuses already ran through my head like a rabid badger on cocaine bouncing off a hundred locked doors in a thousand-mile hallway, trying to find the bathroom.

My legs could be missing. No, he'd probably seen them twitch beneath the covers.

My tongue could be swollen. No, I'd been stupid enough to speak.

I could have a date.

"Like you'd have a date," Gary laughed, reading my mind. The bastard knew me too well.

"Why are you still wearing that stupid hat?" I asked him as the little crocheted balls dangling from his knit cap bounced as he laughed.

"Don't try to change the subject," he said, shaking his finger in my direction. "You know I can't operate the forklift."

I rolled my eyes. "What does Mom want now? There's no way she's out of toilet paper."

"Batteries," Rick said, his grin widening. "She's out of C's."

I laughed, allowing myself to sit up. "Ha," I shouted. "There's a box under the sink."

"Those are D's," Gary said. "We checked."

"Dammit," I cursed out loud, knowing full well I'd blown all chances of getting out of this now.

"See you in the truck," he said over his shoulder as he vanished from my doorway.

I ran my fingers through the hair matted across my scalp. There were a thousand things I'd rather do that day, running all the way from cleaning the sewage pipes with my fingers to licking the avocado green toilet until it turned white. Burying my face in my hands, I sobbed silently. Costco. We were going to Costco.

A million memories flooded my brain. Everything from the four hundred boxes of Cheerios Dad had bought last time to the seven thousand masks we'd bought several months into Covid, all of which turned out to be too small for everyone except Mom. "I can't do this," I whispered into my hands as I sobbed.

"Yes, you can," Gary shouted. "Dad's already revving the engine."

Costco runs were the bane of everyone's existence. My grandparents had been survivors of the Great Depression and passed on their antiquated tendencies to my mother, who had taken to them with a verve known only to the thriftiest of bargain shoppers. We had many times been forced to visit six to nine different grocery stores in a single day (some existing in the adjacent state), just because Mom had tracked down coupons for a vast variety of items we didn't even use, all because it was such a fantastic deal!

Dad, Rick and I had actually hidden the very existence of Costco from her for several years, but a friend from her coupon club had finally spilled the beans.

Dragging myself from the warm covers, I pulled on a pair of jeans, t-shirt and my faded sneakers. I rummaged for my favourite watch for several minutes before realizing I only prolonging the inevitable and grabbed a Casio which would do the job well enough.

"Took you long enough," said Dad, after I'd scaled the ten-foot ladder into the truck and slid in next to Gary. He avoided my glare as I buckled in.

We rode in silence, Dad's grim eyes catching mine in the rear-view mirror on occasion, but he looked away each time. Only Mom seemed in good spirits, which was to say she all but bounced in her seat like a four-year-old on the way to the ice cream shop.

Dad's knuckles turned white as we entered the dreaded parking lot at the North end and made our way to the centre. Rows of empty spaces greeted us at the border, but Mom always insisted we search for spaces closer in. Dad didn't even argue anymore, knowing the fact that we never found one anywhere near the Costco itself was entirely futile, so we began the labyrinth-like circling from the centre out.

A bit like Dante's Inferno, we moved from ring to ring in slow, concentric circles. "There's one," Gary shouted, his voice rising several octaves as he almost broke his pointing finger against the window in excitement.

"That's a cart return," Dad said without glancing over, his voice laboured.

Mom's eyes went wide and she bounced a little again as she signalled another spot.

"Handicap spot," Dad said with a deep sigh, again not even glancing sideways. He knew the parking lot like the back of his hand.

Veteran's spot.

Pregnant woman.

Green vehicles only.

Electric charging station.

Compacts.

Motorcycles.

Cop parking.

A helicopter pad.

Skateboard pile.

Rollerblade bin.

Shoe pile.

Hitching post for horses.

Hoverboard ramp.

Pogo stick holes.

Pigeon feeding station.

"Are there any actual parking spots?" Dad seethed. He slammed on the breaks so hard, Mom nearly went through the windshield. Several spaces up, a red SUV backed out at a snail's pace, as if the driver was just getting used to a backup camera. Facing us, a small sports car revved its engine.

"Don't you dare let him get it," Mom snapped as the SUV inched past the interloper.

"Not a fucking chance," Dad sneered as he floored the truck, spun the wheel and yanked back on the parking brake. Gary and I braced as our gigantic vehicle drifted sideways, barely grazing the vanity plate. SPANKY, was all I saw as we floored it into the fresh spot and slid into place. The enraged driver shot us the finger, but Dad didn't even seem to notice as he switched off the engine and poked his head between the seats. "You guys bring your watches?"

Gary and I brandished our wrist devices.

He slipped a Bluetooth device into his right ear. "Madge," he said, turning to Mom. "Breakfast cereal," he said, gripping her shoulder. She half glanced at him, but didn't seem to be listening. "All you're getting is breakfast cereal."

She gave a weak smile.

"You're not going anywhere near furniture."

"Of course not," she said in a slightly distanced voice as she unlocked her door.

We all remembered the inflatable diving pool she'd bought several years before simply because it had been discounted %60 in an end of Summer blowout sale. The pool was now home to a family of dolphins and one undersized kraken which had somehow found their way into the water receptacle during a very odd Spring.

"Madge," he said, squeezing her shoulder again. "You know I need those Fruit Loops."

"Of course, Sweetheart," she said, without actually glancing over.

Dad gave a deep sigh. "Synchronize watches," he said, clicking the button on his own timepiece. Gary and I followed suite, but he had to set Mom's watch himself. Her eyes looked slightly glazed as she stared out the side window. "Video-phone this time," he added, pulling forth his smartphone. "We've got to stay on contact."

Gary and I were already linked, but Dad had to synch Mom's phone with ours.

"You've got to keep this on, Madge," he said, his stern tone glancing off her glazed exterior.

"Of course, Dear," she said, in muted whisper as she descended the ladder to the parking lot below.

"Boys, try to keep an eye on her," he said as she vanished from sight.

"Sure thing," Gary said, sliding out his door and down the ladder rails.

Dad grabbed my arm as I turned to follow. "Rick," he said, locking eyes with me. "Stay with him this time. We don't need anymore cell phones."

I nodded. Rick had a problem saying no. He'd once dated a girl named Erma Keslington for two years back in elementary just because he'd accidentally passed a note to her from Reggie Biffmartin instead of Margo Marery. We still have some rather adorable pictures of Erma dangling off Gary's shoulder and I torture him with it on special occasions. A postal delivery driver once sold him five hundred stamps he had to pick up at the post office, he once tipped a delivery driver with his own pizza and–as far as we know–he's still legally a Scientologist despite having no money and never attended a meeting. He has most assuredly never actually gone clear.

I gave Dad an exaggerated eye roll and descended after Gary.

The trek from the Outer Reaches took just under and hour, but at long last we stood outside the Costco. The main structure took up just under two city blocks, with several satellites selling party supplies and gardening accoutrements which could be accessed by rail train.

Dad took one massive cart, the approximate size and shape of a steam shovel, while the other three of us were expected to act as runners, dumping our goods in the trough-like implement then making our way back for more.

Per protocol, Dad shoved in first with the cart, blocking off the door lady. We snuck past as he distracted her, rummaging through his wallet. We knew the drill well. He would pull one card out at a time, looking befuddled as possible as he went through every item in his wallet. Driver's license. Credit cards. Diners Card. A vast collection of grocery story reward cards, memberships cards, a Blockbuster card which probably didn't even work at the only Blockbuster store remaining in known reality, his Social Security card, several family pics and a baseball card of Joe Namath. He had a Costco card, of course, but he kept it in the breast pocket of his jacket and only pulled it forth at the last possible moment when the poor lady, who probably just wanted to go home to her children–and the line of shoppers had reached several blocks–had finally begun crying, did he produce said card and present it as if it was the first thing he'd pulled forth from said wallet.

Dad would do all this with a confused smile as if he couldn't remember exactly why he'd stopped in in the first place, and a line of exasperated shoppers had already pushed past in generalized annoyance.

Fun was always had by all–except the poor lady of course–
and we were well past electronics before he'd smiled and
sallied forth. Dad had been the end of more than six greeters
over the years and this explained the series of disguises he
employed in an ever-blossoming attempt to thwart the face
recognition software which already stored over 72 different
mug shots of him dating back to the late 90s.

I ran interference for Gary as we passed the first four or five
kiosks which would have surely sold him air conditioners,
drain covers, aluminium siding, Golden Oldies of the 50s, a
riding lawnmower, a set of galvanized golf clubs, ball bearing
bowling balls, a 1981 Harley Davidson, tickets to The Partridge
Family reunion tour, front row tickets to the next Iowa caucus,
a one-night stay on the International Space Station, a kennel
of massage bunnies, steel rims for his bicycle, an entire leath-
er-bound copy of Strand magazines autographed (via automatic writing) by Sir Arthur Conan Doyle and a grand tour to
the Vatican's first tour of the lower archives.

Gary ran beside me with both fingers buried deep in his
ears as I shouldered the kiosk salespeople aside like an over
steroided line backer. He was crying by the time we made it
to the jewellery section, but heaved a deep sigh of relief as we
reached engagement rings. My brother hadn't dated in several
years, let alone consider matrimony, so we considered that
area an oasis.

"If we can just make it to house wares, I think I'll be okay,"
he said, still heaving a little from all the heavy breathing.

"Damn," I said, glancing up at a Honda generator on the
third shelf above us. The vast shelves extended almost to what

I assumed to be the ceiling so far above I couldn't quite make out where boxes ended. I had to look back down as staring at the ceiling made me dizzy.

Gary glanced up as well. The gleaming piece of machinery stood several feet over our heads.

Only a month before, an ice storm of the likes no one had seen in decades had left us without electricity for almost a week. No cooking. No TV. No video games. Dad had gone into a pseudo-catatonic state because we couldn't recharge the batteries on the Gameboy upon which he liked to play Tetris during his three-hour toilet sessions.

I scratched the back of my head. "Where would we keep it?"

"In the garage," Gary said, trying to keep a straight face.

"Sure," I said. "Because the basement is full."

Dad crackled in my ear. "You boys okay?"

I lifted the phone to my face. "Just checking out the good stuff."

His eyes looked a little wild as massive carts whizzed around him at dizzying speeds. "I'll position myself in the pool toys section and you guys can bring everything to me."

I nodded, knowing the routine all too well. "Gary and I can run interference while Mom does her thing."

"Don't let her get into furniture," Dad snapped. "And don't let Gary near the kiosks."

"Yeah, I know, Dad," I said, giving him my full eye roll. "He's right here."

"Where," asked Dad, apparently glancing at the edges of my screen.

"He's right—shit," I yelled, shoving the phone into my back pocket as I sprinted for the end of the aisle. Gary already stood in front of a cell phone stand, rocking back and forth on his heels with a glassy look on his face.

I flicked my gaze around. Just speaking or even yelling wouldn't work. Gary could ignore just about anything when locked in the grip of just about any salesperson one is likely to ever encounter.

"Would you like sample of pâté on crackers," an old woman croaked from behind one of the thousand make-shift counters which spotted the Costco landscape like LEGO blocks across Gary's floor. Her weak smile looked as if she'd put it on several days before and forgotten to take it off for bed. It sagged at the edges as she listed slightly to the right. Was she mechanical? Possibly. It wouldn't have surprised me if they just packed the sample people away every night.

I twisted to glance up at something. Anything. Once one made eye contact, the jig was generally up. But a light bulb the size of Christmas tree ornament went off in my head and I met her unblinking grey eyes with my wide smile. "Yes," I spat. "God yes." Glancing back at Gary, I could already see the salesgirl moving in for the kill. His eyes were already roving over a collection of variously coloured phones as if he were looking at a collection of candy bars.

The old lady moved mechanically around her little counter as if she'd forgotten how to actually use a spoon. And where the crackers. And what pâté was. And probably why she'd ever agreed to this stupid job in the first place.

"Just one," I said, sounding slightly panicked as she began laying out a row of crackers in tiny paper cups.

Gary had already begun rubbing his chin as his eyes roved the cell phones and cell phone accessories.

"Mmm, that pâté does look good," I said, not so subtly pointing to the open can just to the left of the old woman's elbow. "Can I spread my own?"

The woman's eyes widened like I just turned purple. "You can't touch the spoon, Deary. Covid and all."

I gritted my teeth as Gary made as if to reach for something.

"It's just been so long since I ate," I said, rubbing my stomach to slam the point home. "And I just might buy a vat of that if it's good." I knew good and well she didn't care whether or not I actually bought any, but hoped it might quicken her pace a bit.

She smeared a blob of grey matter onto a square cracker and set it at the end of the row as she reached for the second cracker.

"Thank you," I said, snapping up the cracker and lunging for Gary, whose index finger already rested on a Swiss Army phone case bigger than either his back pockets. "Hey Gar, you gotta try this," I said running the cracker beneath his nose.

Gary's face twitched. His glassy eyes wavered a little as he sniffed the pasty confection. "Phone," he said in a dreamy voice as I moved the cracker away just as he reached for it. "And they have bacon sprinkles just down the way."

He followed me across the aisle, face out way past his toes as if floating along a scent in some Looney Toons sketch. "And you gotta try the cheese balls," I said, as my brother reached for the cracker and I finally let him have it. He scarfed it down with appeared to be more a straight swallow than a chew and swallow. "Cheese balls?" he asked, sniffing at the air like a dog trying to find the scent of green Frisbee.

"Shit," I spat, yanking my phone from my pocket and bringing the screen to bear. "Mom," I yelled into the blank square. "Mom, where are you?"

It took several seconds for her muffled voice to come over the phone. "Just looking for Fruit Loops, dear," she said, light poking through edges of the frame, bits of warm pink showing through.

"Mom, why can't I see you?" I shouted.

Gary was filling his face with cheese balls from a canister the approximate size and shape of an apple barrel.

"I just don't know how to make the phone work," she said in an odd tone as if her hand had been caught in the coupon cookie jar. "Oh, I really don't like this one. Where's the camera. I can't see you, dear."

I groaned, trying to gauge her location by the wisps of light making their way around what I was fairly was her finger. "That doesn't look like the cereal aisle," I said, glimpsing what appeared to be an inflatable alligator dangling from a yellow net.

"I can't hear you, dear," she said, voice dripping with honey sweetness. "Gotta go. I think there's a full bin of Honey Bunches of O's over here for half price."

I sighed. Mom couldn't pass up a deal if it sat in the middle of a bear trap illuminated by a spotlight in the ceiling. Dammit, I thought, scanning the aisles for Gary. He'd vanished already. This time I grabbed a several samples of honey mustard pretzels and walked the aisles calling his name.

This was not going well. We'd been there over an hour and hadn't pinned down a single item. At that moment I was very glad Dad had the only cart as I darted from row to row, shaking the bag of pretzels in front of me in the hope the sound might attract his attention. Had he got hungry and headed to the food court?

Rounding a corner, the entire toilet paper aisle spread out before me like a fluffy white wonderland. Hmm, I thought. How were we doing on toilet paper?

The clack clack of a shotgun sounded several feet away. I whirled to see Old Man Winters sitting on ten-foot pile of Charmin. "This ain't the place for you, the old man said, levelling the massive hand canon on me from his elevated position.

Apparently Old Man Winters still hadn't quite forgot our toilet paper prank, despite the fact that we'd later purchased massive amounts from him the following year when COVID struck.

I turned the corners up on my mouth in a placating grin and backed away. At least I knew Gary must not have come this way, so I slipped back around the corner, hands still in the air. It looked as if the next time we needed massive amounts of TP, we'd have to go to Sam's Club.

Gary tapped me on the shoulder. "You gotta try these cupcakes," he said, white frosting still smeared his left cheek.

"Don't come this way," I said, leading him back down towards groceries. "Looks like someone's still peeved about our toilet paper escapade."

"No sense of humour," Gary said, licking bits of frosting off his fingers. "Should we tell him the skunks in his cellar were us?"

I raised an eyebrow, remembering the shotgun. "Maybe better than telling him about the porcupine we stuffed through his bathroom window."

He nodded. "Better grab something to put in Dad's cart so he thinks we're actually doing something."

"Oranges?" I asked, pointing to a display the mass of a mid-sized SUV.

"I like oranges," Gary said, rolling up his sleeves.

We carried a bulk the approximate shape of an industrial garbage bag. Dad had already exchanged the cart for a six-wheel flatbed with all terrain tires. "Where did you find that?" I asked as we piled the oranges onto a massive box of LED light bulbs.

"My secret," Dad said, with a grin. "Where's your mother?"

"Still buying Fruit Loops, last I checked."

Dad sighed. "She hasn't been answering her phone."

"Uh, yeah," I said, running my fingers through my hair, trying to look ignorant. "She seems to be having trouble using her phone."

"She can use it better than me," he said, clenching the rubber grips on the flatbed handle which came almost up to his neck.

I shrugged. "We can get her on the way to checkout," I said, taking the left side of the handle as Dad took the right. The flatbed was piled so high we had to use bungees to keep it all from tumbling over and killing small children on our way.

"Have Gary keep the bags of rice from dragging on the front," he said as we leaned into the handle. Once we got it going, momentum seemed to keep us moving.

"Gary?" I asked, glancing around. "Where is Gary?"

My stomach went cold as we turned to see the white tassels of Gary's hat bobbing up and down several hundred feet away at the cell phone kiosk. The lady there was pointing to something on the screen of her tablet as Gary reached his finger towards it.

Time slowed as Dad screamed the word, "nooooooooooooooo," and I broke into a flat sprint. I dodged carts and shoppers, vaulting an electric piano and sloloming barrels of chocolates. There was a rush of wind as I leapt, flying towards my brother like an NFL linebacker and tackling him just as his finger touched the tablet.

Gary struggled against me from underneath as I pinned him to the floor. "You don't need another phone, man," I said, gripping his flailing arms.

The kiosk lady stared down at us with eyes as big as UFOs. "He was just buying insurance," she said, trying to force a smile across her stunned features.

"Goddammit," I spat, dragging Gary to his feet and shoving him towards Dad, "he doesn't need anymore insurance. He's already got three warranties on all his phones."

Dad took one arm and I grabbed the other as we led him back to the cart. "She was so cute," said Gary as we locked him between us at the flatbed handle. "It was only going to cost twenty dollars a month—"

"For the rest of your life?" I asked.

"Twenty years," said Gary with a heavy shrug.

"Your phone won't last twenty years," I seethed. "Dude, you gotta stay away from those things."

"I know," Gary said, shuffling his feet as we pushed past the furniture section. "But she was soooo cute."

Dad gave out an audible gulp and we stopped to see what he was looking at. Mom stood grinning her peroxide smile as she sat in the centre of a huge L shaped sofa.

"Madge, you promised," Dad said, on the verge of tears.

"It's on sale," she said, spreading her arms. "And it comes with an ottoman and matching easy chair."

We spent the next half hour wrapping the results of our shopping onto pallets and forklifting then into place on the truck. The new living room set had to be strapped to the roof with a series of ropes and bungee cords of such complexity I doubted we'd be able to undo them with anything less than a pair of hedge trimmers.

Dad gripped the steering wheel like he wanted to break it in two as Mom beamed beside him. "Dammit, Madge," he said through gritted teeth. "You didn't even get the Fruit Loops."

Gary huddled in the corner appearing to sleep, but he seemed to be fiddling with something beneath his jacket. "What the Hell, Ger?" I asked, yanking the denim folds open to reveal something cradled in his hands.

My brother recoiled, closing his fingers around a rectangular object with more bling on it than Cadillac license plate. He grinned at me sheepishly. "I got another phone."

Blue Light

Andrew W. McCollough

The whole thing started a few months back as the long winter crossed its arms and decided to get darker, rainier, and even more depressing than usual. Right after Dana's girlfriend dumped him just before the holidays.

"Statistically, the most common time", said @GoatFer, one of his guildies, "Better to dump the boyfriend now then spend the holidays with someone you are planning to dump. Cleaner. Fuck!Kill that troll." Dana winced as @GoatFer's mic popped.

"On it," He thwacked the troll viciously with a longsword he kept for that purpose. "Still, unnecessarily harsh though. Winters are long." The longsword cleaved the troll in half and then sent a burst of sparkles across the screen. The troll dropped no loot at all, not even a bag of copper.

"Think of it as your chance to level up, Dingbat." Dana thought the handle was clever when he'd thought of it. Not so much ten years later.

Anyway, he didn't want to level up, the level had been fine already. At least for him. She had had a different opinion, obviously. "I am leveling, this quest will bring me to level 65 at least."

"Not that, your obsession with people. Connection. Alone time is good for people like us."

"I'm not obsessed, we're social animals." Or would be if he could socialize without a panic attack.

"Maybe you are, but I'm over it now. And happier."

"What do you mean?" Dana asked, but @GoatFer didn't reply except to point out more trolls.

The guildies meant well but their advice didn't help. Nothing helped except two, three, four, six day sessions raiding orc nests as he played-tested the latest in-game expansion. The two weeks following the release he played until his crappy Sony monitor pixelated to death and @GoatFer, the only other guildie at Blaze, the game company he QA'd for, requisitioned an enormous new monitor for him. An experimental OLED screen, @GoatFer said, designed to support extended play–maybe it could help him out. Dana didn't think a new monitor could wipe the memory of his most recent romantic crash, but @GoatFer insisted.

The monitor really did support extended play. The monitor glowed a particular actinic blue that pained his eyes at first but the more he played the more he appreciated the crisp edges, vivid colors, and palpable warmth the monitor exuded. More than once he caught himself leaning so close to the screen that the skin of his face tightened from the heat, eyes wide, sucking in the photons that the clouded winter sky outside denied him.

And as the deadline for the expansion hurtled toward him and he found himself playing until his clicking hand went numb from the little finger to the middle of his hand and down to his elbow. Playing until the gamer funk made the pizza delivery guy wince. Playing until he realized that it had been three days since he'd last ordered pizza and he wasn't really hungry anyway and besides, he felt fine.

Really, just fine.

Not like he'd just been gutted, or dumped out of a moving van, or tossed on the scrap heap of ex-life-partners. Fine.

Better than he had any right to expect, better, really, than he had ever felt before in the sturm und drang of past relationships all the way back to his ur-loves as a child. This purely fine existence felt like more than he deserved. No more, no less.

The neighbor cursing through the wall penetrated the white noise from his headphones. Then the wall shook as something about the weight of a forcefully thrown internet router thudded against the far side. The wilting plant hanging just out of reach of sunlight in the corner of the kitchen swayed and a dry leaf wafted to the table. The stale loaf of bread nudged off the counter, fell to the floor, and broke in half.

Greta had moved in six months prior and had unfortunately chosen Concast as her ISP. As if she had a choice. In that time, Concast had repeatedly forgotten that her ex-boyfriend was no longer at the address and turned her off for his non-payment. She could usually get them to turn it on after a few days on the customer care line, but once it had been a full week of her shouting on the phone in the morning and then working at the café on the corner the rest of the day.

Dana adjusted his custom-fitted headphones and turned up the volume. Blaze Corp intended to release the Troll

Tromp expansion in three months and he had yet to finish the first three quests. Definitely looked like death march grind days coming. Yet the prospect did not fill him with the same dread that it had in the past. Now, grinding meant even more screen photons washing over him in a cleansing blue mist that floated away every distraction. The Blaze Corp monitor, delivered complements of @GoatFer, helped tremendously.

"He doesn't live here anymore!" The subsequent thud of what was likely her mobile phone made him wince. He needed to finish two quests this week to stay on track. He checked his internet speed; plenty fast, much more than he needed. One of the perks of the job meant having a home connection at business bandwidth. He spent another five minutes psyching himself into social contact, then went upstairs.

Greta opened at his knock "What?" she jammed her fingers at her phone, miraculously still working, and frowned up at him, "I'm busy here."

"Yeah, I heard."

"Surprised by that, thought you glued your earphones to you head."

He ignored that, he really just didn't have the energy. "Look, while you're waiting for Concast to turn your internet back on, why don't you just use mine? I'll give you the password and you can surf to your heart's content."

"No, thanks. I can get my own. There's Presso right downstairs."

"Concast can take weeks to come through and you can't hang in the café all day. It honestly doesn't matter to me, my company pays, but . . ."

"But at least you'll have fewer shouting matches next door."

"Yeah." He hadn't wanted to say it but, fuck. "It got loud. Not that I blame you, but I have to work too."

She shrugged and took the password, letting him get back to his monitors. The reassuring blue helped slow his heart. Dana wiped his palms dry on his sweats and pressed one hand against the soothing fuzz on his screen. Breathe, count 1,2,3,4,5 breathe. This would be fine. Even if her machine were a seething pit of malware he used a VPN. He and the game would be safe on the other side of a secure, 256 bit encrypted tunnel. His palm tingled pleasantly and he sat forward in his chair, closer to his gaming screen.

Now, where were those trolls?

Two days later Dana had almost finished killing a particularly obnoxious troll in a penultimate quest thread when the knocking on the door distracted him a precisely the right moment for the troll to kill him. This is why he didn't like people. He ripped open the door, his irritation enough that he almost didn't feel terrified that Greta stood so close, standing at the door with a cookie sitting on a napkin in her hand.

"What?" he snapped.

Greta took a step back, "A cookie? From Presso? A thank-you for your wifi password?"

"Ah, no. " The cookie was the color of old pus speckled with black flecks, "I really don't eat much."

"You can't say no to a chocolate chip cookie!"

Dana felt the fragile safety-bubble around him tremble. He

didn't want the cookie but he couldn't figure a way to refuse. He took the cookie.

"What's going on in there?" She looked past him, "Looks like you're opening a movie theatre or something."

"No, just work. I need the screens."

"Looks more like you're the star of an interrogation."

He turned around and for the first time in a while really saw his room. His workstation stood against the wall, surrounded on all sides by looming monitors turned to maximum brightness. The Blaze Corp screen, a 90-inch monster, dominated the others like the sun over moons. His chair crouched under them, the intoxicating smell of warm plastic rising from it.

"You sure you don't want a snack break? Overwork will kill you."

Dana hesitated to tell her as it sounded crazy even to him. No thanks, I just lean close to my computer screen and it gives me all the energy I need. She'd think he was crazy for sure. And maybe he was, couldn't say. But what was true was that he didn't need to eat.

"Uh, well," and he found himself telling her the whole story. She shook her head.

"That explains why I haven't even heard the pizza guy recently." The youngest pizza box in the stack on the kitchen counter was two months old.

"Yeah, really good way to save. Electricity is much cheaper than food."

"You really don't eat anything at all?"

"I've heard of yogis going years without eating, so it isn't impossible."

"Well, maybe, but no offense, Dana, you're no yogi."

"Not a traditional one, maybe. But what if there are other ways of becoming a yogi? Other ways of reaching that level of detachment and mental control?"

"Sounds plausible. Like what? What skills do you have you haven't told me?"

"I'm a professional game player."

"Like the competitive e-sport guys?

"Not one of competitive ones, no. I play-test."

"Fun." She did not seem convinced that effective play-testing required a yogi-level of mental control. "Well, hope you figure out what is going on. Can't be healthy."

She gave him the cookie anyway, 'just in case', and he set it, wrapped in a brown napkin, beside the sink. He meant to throw it away, but after the first couple of days the smell blended with the pervasive scent of hot plastic into a faint chocolate and sugar scent that reminded him of the specialty erasers he used in grade school math class three decades prior.

He let it stay.

The encounter with Greta and her reaction made Dana curious about his condition. Were there others like him? Was he really a yogi and eating photons from his screens? If so, how had that happened? He'd done yoga with his ex once, sitting stiffly in newly-purchased, too-small sweatpants on sour-smelling mats while an overly cheerful instructor gracefully bent into a q-shape. Dana had very ungracefully fallen over and rolled off of his mat. He'd stopped going after the second week, citing work.

His long-dusty question engine coughed and began to turn over. His state really was not in any sense normal. And likely broke several of what he'd thought were inviolable biological laws. Eat, Breathe, Sleep, Shit, Repeat were basic, and he'd managed to somehow get around two of those. And truth be told, he slept less and less as well, hardly more than four hours a night, most nights. A thin, wailing emotion that could have once been fear twitched feebly in the vicinity of his stomach. Maybe he should look into it, do a bit of research, see if anything turned up.

He managed to procrastinate any actual research for a few more weeks, but the weirdness built into a panic that settled into his chest and squeezed his lungs hard whenever he inadvertently found himself pressing his face and hands against the flickering screen. Worse, it felt so...good. Felt like it was all he needed. Felt cool and calm and completely drama-less. Felt perfectly fine.

He ran a few cursory searches and found rumors supporting his photon theory. Yogis claiming to live on sunlight. Reports of Zen monks subsisting on nothing but water and meditation for years. Even some unsubstantiated rumors of Silicon Valley startup programmers spending days in tech-bro-funk caves only emerging into the SF fog for coffee when the RedBull kegs ran dry. Suggestions, but nothing concrete.

But in the Reddit lairs and usenet forums one name kept coming up. Japsar, no last name. Always in connection to breatharians, or light-eaters, or etherphagic practitioners. It took him some time but he ran the guy down, a local, and managed to set a meet at the nearest MacD.

★

Dana navigated to the meet better than usual. Maybe this light thing was good for him? The ten minute bus ride felt interminable, but his mirror shades, ball cap, and oversized pair of what he called "outside" headphones cranked to 10 kept an almost-comfortable clear space around him.

Japsar sat at the back near the playground drinking a tall paper cup of something fizzy and likely very sweet through a straw in long slurps. He waved Dana down.

Clearly, whatever connection Japsar had to this it wasn't the light-eating. Two double-stack burgers oozing neon-yellow cheese squatted next to a double-wide carton of perfectly crisp fries, an empty box of nuggets, and a discarded fish-sandwich wrapper.

"Surf&Turf McD style," Japsar mumbled and nudged the spilling cornucopia of fries at him. Dana shook his head and sat down.

"Looks good," he said, "No thanks. I've just eaten."

"Have you?" Japsar slurped at him and set the cup down. "Then why bother to see me?"

"Just being polite. The thought actually disgusts me." It was all Dana could do not to dry-heave all over the day-glow orange table.

"Good. Thought I was wasting my time for a moment."

An employee wearing a ridiculous paper hat set another orange tray on the table. Three candy apple pies and a double-fudge sundae drooling chocolate over the side of the plastic bowl.

"Sorry, spilled it, " the employee muttered.

"Just don't forget dessert, later," said Japsar and dipped his fry in the chocolate puddle. The employee backed away and then fled through the flapping doors behind the counter.

"I didn't know McD had table service."

"Anyplace does if you tip enough. I tip enough."

"Guess so. Tell me, what do you know about this? This light-eating?"

"No business before dinner. And don't say that out loud."

"Why not?"

Japsar didn't answer, just unwrapped the second double-decker and ate. Dana had nothing else he wanted to ask Japsar so the two sat staring at each other as Japsar steadily chewed through the burger, swallowed the last bite, then opened the next.

The monotonous chomp of Japsar's jaws, the insidious convulsions of his throat, the wet smack of his mouth grated on Dana until he stood up and walked out to the playground. Listening to that almost malicious chewing was more than he could stand. He walked around the looping stack of the lavender playground tube slide, watching Japsar through the shatter-proof glass, until the second burger, the fries, the sundae, and all three pies were gone, before coming back in.

"Ready to talk?"

"Sure, sit," Japsar sat back wiping his mouth on a handful of napkins, "Let's run through the questions." He pulled a razor-thin clamshell out of his backpack and snapped it open on the table. The screen lit with a tasty azure glow that even in the backwash off of Japsar's face felt good. Dana involuntarily leaned closer to absorb some of it. He could see the startup screen in Japsar's glasses flash a bland corporate logo, a big blue circle enclosing concentric triangle, square, and circle. Below a similarly bland slogan, ".erutuF rethgirB a evlovE". Something about the logo looked familiar, but he couldn't place it. A gaming console? Maybe a controller logo?

Japsar looked at him sharply and adjusted the laptop. "No peeking. I'll tell you now, there is someone you must go see if you want to know the truth. What is really going on, who is really behind it, what the final result is. But the question you need to ask yourself is, do you really want to know? You can't unlearn it. Once you are in, you're in. Are you ready for that?"

"I don't know, I think I am."

"Weak sauce response, Dana. Not good enough at all." Jasper snapped his clamshell closed and pushed back his chair. "You won't see me again."

"No wait, just a second." Dana grabbed Jasper's arm, the thick sweater dampening under his clammy grip. "I am ready, I've got to know. This whole thing has me freaked out. I'm not sure what is happening to me and I don't know what is next. Please, help me."

Jasper looked down at the hand on his sleeve. "Hands off, D. You know the rules."

"Sorry, sorry." Dana let him go and sank back into his yellow plastic bucket chair, "Will you help?"

"You don't sound ready, just desperate. Until you are, giving you this info will just damage you."

"I am ready, really."

"You don't even know what the info is."

"I know enough. Know that I'm changing, have already changed. It's been three months."

Jasper bent down and looked into Dana's left pupil. "How long, exactly?"

"Three months, two days, and about seven hours since I last ate or drank anything. Got rained on on the way here, but didn't swallow."

"Hmm," Jasper sat down and scooched his metal frame chair back under the table, leaned toward Dana. "Your pupils are right about the three month stage. Show me your hands."

"There are stages?" Dana leaned toward Jasper but managed to stop himself this time from touching him. Japsar produced a thin metal wand from his pocket, grabbed his right hand and turned it over, palm up, prodding with the probe.

"Yes. From what you just said, you look to be stage two, maybe early three. Ah, dessert!" The employee was back with yet another tray overflowing fries. The employee set a full tub of ketchup on the table.

"How many stages are there?"

"Several. But I'm not going to let you pump me for info, D. My job is simple: I decide whether I tell you what I know." Jasper sat back, picked a long yellow fry crisped golden brown along one square-cut edge, doodled it through the ketchup tub, then delicately bit off the end. He chewed, dipped again, then with his jaw chomping furiously he pushed the rest of the fry into his mouth like a limb going into a wood chipper.

Dana's throat convulsed and if there were anything in his stomach he was sure it would have come out. He used to do that. Chew. Unbelievable. He turned his head and watched the clown on the video screen above the register chase burger thieves. The screen was too far for nourishment and he'd seen the show before, but it comforted him. The chomping and slurping went on and on, like a hand rubbing over rough concrete. Finally Jasper sighed, picked up his soda, and leaned back.

Jasper waited to speak until after a long pull on the soda. "D. You've got physical signs, I'll give you that. But you know, you just aren't mentally there. Can't help you." He stuffed his clamshell into his backpack and stood up again.

"You're not going to help?"

"No. Some people get it right away, some take years. You'll know when you do. Call me then, we'll talk." He spun on his sneaker heel and left.

Years? There was no way Dana could wait years to find out what was going on. What the next step was. What was actually happening to him. Now that he was curious, the curiosity was burning through the stretched bubble of complacency that had protected him. He wouldn't quit now. Couldn't.

He was going to find out. Fortunately, Jasper had left him a lead to go on, even if accidentally. Dana didn't have a name, but he had a logo, and that might be good enough.

It wasn't good enough. Not that his crap artistic skills helped much, but even he could Photoshop together the superimposed circle, square, and triangle he'd seen in Japsar's glasses and run an image search on the web. He found a few pics that looked similar, but none of them tied back to any company he could find. The closest results matched an ancient alchemical symbol for the philosopher's stone, a magical substance that could transmute lead into gold and confer immortality. Not helpful.

The slogan had the opposite problem. There were at least 1500 companies world wide claiming to create, build, or make a brighter future. None that were evolving one.

Three days of fruitless internet searches and he almost considered going down to the library to consult paper, a sign of true desperation. Not everything, not quite yet, was on the net. He was willing to a take a risk on an unconventional research approach and eventually bought several books of esoterica on Amazon.

He ran into Greta week later on an infrequent trip down to the mailboxes to check on his Amazon deliveries. Two books and a new pro mouse had arrived.

"You eat that cookie yet?"

"No, not really. Smells good"

"Its been three weeks. I don't think it smells like anything."

"To me it does." He shrugged.

"You want to get coffee? I'm heading out to the Café Presso."

"Nah, I got work. Big release coming up and I've got to get the reviews back."

"Fucking corporations will kill you. You're not looking that great. Kinda pasty. Your eyes . . . are you sleeping? Can't work if you're dead, you know."

"Hah."

"Happened to a friend. That is why I tapped out."

"I'm fine." And it was true, so far as it went. He was just fine.

She shrugged and continued down the stairs."Bang on the door if you change your mind, Dana. Later."

He wouldn't change his mind, couldn't change his mind. In fact, his mind ran away from him and he had no control of it at all. He almost dropped the small Amazon box in his hand and he realized he was leaning against the peeling metal wall of the stairwell gawping like a fish on the bank waiting blunt trauma to his head.

He'd had enough. Too much. Japsar, Greta, this whole weird thing with his body. Dana felt his breathing shallow and panicked and the world flickered at the edges. He needed screen time.

His computer hummed, the heat breathing from under his desk as comforting as the memory of hot chocolate. He plugged in the new mouse and surfed to a streaming video site, skimming through offerings until he found a show he hadn't consumed before. Multiple simultaneous episodes spilled across his screens at triple play-back speed. He zoned in. The mouse clicks crisp and precise, the pointer tracked smooth as butter. He leaned close and pressed his cheek against the smooth smooth glass, spread his fingers over the warm screen, closed his eyes, and basked.

Greta's door slamming startled him away from the screen, the clock in the corner showed he'd lost three hours. His shirt hung open, he'd had his chest pressed against the monitor, embracing it. His face hurt and he ran a finger over the welted edge his monitor had left on his cheek. Nearly midnight and he had neither finished a quest or was any closer to finding Japsar. He picked at the crust in his eyes then stumbled into the bathroom to wash his face. He had work to do tonight.

Dana squeezed his eyes shut against the flickering fluorescents. Funny how the monitor didn't bother him, if anything the opposite, but the white light in the bathroom pained. Greta had been right, he did look sick, with purple half-moons under his eyes, his skin, never healthy-looking, turned pasty, splotched gray and white, with a grease-slick patina. He felt his breath coming short and he took a breath and held it as long as he could, until his panicked gawping emerged into a full yawn and settled him, for now.

On an impulse he couldn't quite identify Dana cracked the door as Greta came stamping back up the stairs.

"Hey, can I bounce some ideas off you?"

"It's late Dana, I'm not in the mood."

"Two minutes. I just need a second opinion." Weeks of churning in circles, staring at a seemingly endless stream of esoteric glyphs was getting to him.

"Just a second," He dodged back into the living room and swung his monitor around toward the door, showing her the symbol. "Does this remind you of anything?"

"High school geometry class," she shrugged, then frowned,"Now that I think about it, it does remind me of that company my friend used to work for. Q something."

"Q? Can you remember more than that? Your friend?" Was this actually a lead?

"Quintas" But she couldn't tell him anything more.

After she left he sat back down and reached toward his monitor to move it back into place. A pattern on the lower edge near the power cable caught his eye and he frowned, pulled the monitor closer on its mechanical arm. Not just any pattern, a superimposed square, circle, and triangle. The same alchemical symbol he'd been staring at for days. He'd thought he'd seen it before, and he had, while setting up his new monitor from Blaze. The one his guildie had requisitioned for him. But what would Blaze have to do with Quintas?

Even with the name Greta gave him and the connection to Blaze the search took until nearly four AM before he'd located the building he'd seen in Japsar's screen. Nothing moved in the streets at four AM, too late for drunks, even the wandering street dwellers were bedded down on whatever square of cardboard they could find.

A stumbling late-night drunk party goer let him into the building and he took the elevator to the basement. With nearly one hundred apartments in the building he had no hope of finding the one he wanted by chance and he could hardly go knocking on each door at this hour.

But the basement held a rack of electrical meters, one for each apartment. Nearly four in the morning and only one apartment showed a steady tick-tick of the power running. Someone was up late and using a lot of electricity. The number scrawled in grease pencil on the meter read 5D.

The hall lights on 5 trembled, half of the fluorescent tubes dying, the others already dead. A familiar blue glow seeped from under the gray-painted door and reflected off the streaked linoleum flooring.

This was it. He would finally know, would see. This room would reveal what he was becoming, what he could be. Dana wasn't sure whether the fear or the excitement churned his guts the most. He tried the door, unlocked, and he hesitated, hand on the dented steel bulb. Was he really ready? Did he want to know what he was becoming?

But if he left now he would never have the courage to come back.

He pushed open the heavy steel door.

The opening door flooded a flickering glow through the hallway. The blue soaked into his skin, into his ears, his eyes, the flicker spreading a calming numbness across his bones and settling the ache buried in his chest.

A naked figure sat silhouetted against a wall-sized screen. A wall made up of screens, Dana realized, each tuned to a different channel or to none at all, so white noise and flickering blue hash filled the room. The goblin's hands pressed to the screen in front of him. The fingers spread moistly, webbed, pallid, spatulate against the flickering glass like enormous frog toes. His back slicked with a viscous fluid that oozed down him, sogged his briefs, and formed a shallow pool on the linoleum. A slow shift in his posture, a sliding hand leaving a snail-trail glistening on the glass, made a faint squelching sound and small ripples shuddered on the surface of the slime he sat in. His skin glistened the static blue from the screens around him.

The figure turned its head and pressed a bulging cheek against the screen like a lover. Its eyes, globular and staring, the same blank blue of the screen, blinked slowly, half-lidded. A scar, twisted and inflamed, writhed across the left side of its face. Dana, startled in a sickening realization, made an involuntary squeak like that of a mouse snatched up by a snake.

One eye turned toward him, rotating like that of a chameleon, the other still and staring straight at the wall. The globulous eye widened, the white pupil dilating, then it constricted again. Its throat convulsed, cheeks working, and it seemed to be trying to suck enough moisture into its mouth to speak. Then, belying the dampness of its skin, a voice dry as sand croaked, "Dingbat . . ."

The door handle slipped from his sweating hands and the heavy began to swing closed against him, pushing him from the room.

"Don't go . . ."

The door slipped from his suddenly damp palms and slammed shut, breaking whatever curse had held him paralyzed. Dana turned and ran and didn't stop until he was shaking under his bedsheet and even then his mind spun like a hamster trapped on his doomed wheel.

This early Presso's outside tables were empty. He set his phone, screen down, on the white tablecloth, his tablet and laptop secured in his zippered and locked bag. The screens were there, tempting, but the thought of a future in a white tiled room filled with an empty blue glow cramped his stomach every time he reached for one. He might need a new job.

His hands wrapped tight around the cheap ceramic mug, coffee unsipped, but the heat warmed his hands. Greta waved at him from the counter.

"Thanks for coming."

"No worries, did you find what you were looking for?" Greta sat opposite him under the umbrella's shade at the bistro table and set her coffee and pastry onto the table.

"In a manner of speaking." The coffee trembled when he set it down and it rattled against the wire mesh under the cheap cloth. He hadn't been able to stop the shaking in his hands, not since last night. "I found out where this thing is going."

"Oh?" She ripped a corner of the croissant and chewed slowly.

"Yes, uh, nowhere good." He told her everything, how it had started, his initial suspicions, the meeting with Japsar, and what he had seen in the abandoned apartment complex. "I don't doubt that was @GoatFer, what was left of him, what he'd become. I think that is happening to me." He held out a pasty hand, damp fingers spread and spatulate as a gecko's. "Look."

She swallowed the fragment of the croissant and sipped her coffee. "If you don't want to become that don't. Do something different."

"But what?"

"Not really my field. But I'd suggest look at everything that got you here and do the opposite. For instance."

She pushed the plate and croissant toward him.

"Have some."

The croissant glowed a rich brown, even in the shade, each layer flaking light and delicate and crisp as autumn leaves and shedding the scent of browned butter into his awareness like rich smoke. A white plastic ramekin still cradled a swirl of lemon curd that glistened sour-sweet yellow. Thick saliva pooled in his mouth and for the first time in months he considered eating. He didn't even know if he could, it had been so long. He looked up, questioning, not sure even what he wanted to ask. "Do you think...can I?"

Greta smiled and her eyes crinkled, "Go on."

The croissant rustled but tore easily, butter yellow and white shreds gesturing slowly in the air while its brown crust shed a season of golden-brown flakes to the plate.

He could stay as he was, just fine. Take only enough screen time to stay alive but not enough to complete his transformation. But there was something beyond fine and for the first time in over a year he was interested in finding out what that was.

He held the fragment of croissant in his hand, warm butter slicking his fingers, and took a bite.

The Way You Taste

Jessie Kwak

Something tastes wrong about the Hinojosas' living room tonight. Harney pauses at the edge of his frame, tongue flicking the air as he tries to suss out just what it is.

He drinks deep of the thing he's come for: Adriana Leon de Hinojosa's most recent lie to cover up her affair, layered over the rest of the family's tangled net of tensions like a rich, bitter-salty chocolate. And that's when he realizes: This emotion may be fresh, but someone else has tasted it first.

He nearly loses his connection to the Hinojosa home entirely; the sound of an old woman's snores and a crying baby two rows back try to edge in at his consciousness. Harney pushes them away and slips back into the frame.

Drinks in the room.

He tastes passionate citrus splashes of pure affection from the youngest daughter. The raging, sour indifference of the oldest daughter, the delectable see-sawing insecurities of the middle son. The Hinojosa family's emotions are made intoxicatingly complex by the depth of their mutual love—even Adriana's infidelity isn't simple, like some of the others he's tasted. It's tortured and passionate and unwilling, steeped ever stronger over the past month as she knows her husband has begun to suspect what's happening, but she still can't seem to stop herself.

It's the strongest emotion he's tasted—or felt—in a decade.

And someone else is here, sampling a feast that should be his alone.

He scans the room for the interloper and finally finds something out of place on the coffee table: a framed photo from the family's recent trip to Paris.

Eiffel Tower in the background, fringed with lacy pink blossoms, the Hinojosa family with arms around each other in the foreground.

And behind them? A woman: long, glossy black hair and a simple green dress, pretending to study a map. Oblivious to the tourists around her, you would think. But she's not looking at the map at all. Her eyes are boring straight into the camera, over Adriana's shoulder.

The shock of the realization sends Harney out of the Hinojosa living room entirely, and he flinches so hard in his tiny airplane seat that the old woman beside him snuffles half awake.

It can't be.

The woman in the photo?

She's just like him.

Three months later it happens again.

Harney slips into Nairobi, into the living room of a couple he first spotted on their honeymoon last year in Barcelona. They were clearly in love in front of La Sagrada Familia, giddy newlywed joy wafting in cinnamon-sugar clouds that he used to savor, but now finds sickly sweet and boring. When they walked by, though, some fear-spice in the undercurrent caught his attention.

He'd slipped behind them as though to get a closer look at the church's jumbled spires, tasting the faint anguished chatter from the boy: I love her, but I'm in love with him.

The girl's pure joy blending smooth with the acidic, dynamic tang of the boy's anxiety was intoxicating.

Harney had slipped behind them when they'd asked another tourist clumsily to tomar un foto and his soul splintered as the shutter snapped shut.

(It hurts every time, like being sliced through with a blade so razor-sharp your body doesn't know at first the cut's been made.)

Now, in Nairobi, the couple are sitting down to dinner with the girl's brother, and the boy and the brother are both desperately pretending the magnetic draw between their souls doesn't exist. The exquisite blend of desire and disappointment and crushing weight is sweet and heady as any liqueur, but Harney barely notices. Someone else has sipped of this scene before Harney could arrive.

Harney scans the room again and sees it: Paris, the steps of the Notre-Dame, the dark haired woman. He studies her from his own frame. She's bold; whereas Harney always tries to make his eye contact with the camera subtle, she's staring right at the lens once more, lips curled up in a secret smile.

He jolts awake in his Brisbane hotel room, the raucous sound of bars spilling out into the streets below. He throws aside sheets soaked through in sweat, pulls out his laptop, and books a flight.

★

On the flight to Paris, he sleeps and he scans.

He rarely visits his favorites more than once every few months, but now Harney sweeps through them in a gluttonous rush that leaves him both jittery and somehow even hungrier than when he started. He takes inventory, paying special attention to the ones who tend to travel the most and always display the photos.

He finds her in a living room in Buenos Aires, a child's bedroom in Wichita, a kitchen in Seoul—all photos from trips to Paris, all from the last few months and weeks.

Harney adores Paris. The capital of complicated emotion, it's the destination for terrified new lovers, jilted and bitter rebounds, bittersweet dying wishes. Tourists from around the world, each bringing their unspeakable hopes and secrets and fears and lies with them, streaming past the tourist hot spots like fish in a stream.

When he'd hunted Paris, he'd preferred the historic cafes of Montmartre, a few hours spent over a coffee at a sidewalk table always granted opportunities to appear in the photos of tortured artists fueling their own insecurities by visiting the places where the greats drank themselves into spectacular bonfires.

She prefers Place du Trocadero; it's easy hunting with the tourists always trying multiple angles to get the Eiffel Tower in the background. So when he arrives in Paris that's where he directs the taxi driver.

He's prepared for the overwhelming wave of emotion as he steps out into the square, his overnight bag slung over his shoulder. But something is different this time—the residual jitters from his binge on the plane, maybe. Now, where he normally takes only the tiniest sips until he finds an emotion to collect, he can't help but gulp at anyone who comes too close.

He scans the plaza, so intent on finding the woman and dizzy from the glut he is taking in that he doesn't noticed the approaching tour group until they have surrounded him.

I'm afraid, I'm alone, I don't understand, I'm a fraud, I'm dying, I miss her, I should have told him, I'll do better next time, I'm desperate—

Harney's on his knees, spinning in the storm, fighting off crushing dark and gasping for breath.

"Buddy, you all right?"

A man in a Yankees baseball cap is guiding him to a bench, offering him a bottle of water, and Harney latches onto the uncomplicated caramel buzz of boredom from this man who is dutifully checking Paris off his wife's bucket list for their twenty-eighth anniversary.

"Thanks," Harney says. "Came here straight from the airport, and I think I'm a little jet lagged."

"I can never sleep on planes," the man says amicably, patting Harney on the arm and getting to his feet. "Hate 'em. Enjoy Paris!"

Harney sits on the bench sipping water for an hour before he feels able to brave the crowd again.

He does not see the woman, but when he allows himself to carefully taste from the passersby, he catches a faint dark print of her presence on their psyches.

She was here. Only moments before.

★

Three days later he finally spots her, back in the Trocadero.

She's hunting a group of girlfriends from São Paulo, and he can see why she's chosen them. One is secretly pregnant and desperately trying to fake happiness for the camera while she decides what to do about it, and Harney catches the pungent sweet-and-acrid blend of her forced smiles and terror before he even spots the girl herself.

He slips behind the dark-haired woman, pretending to check his watch as the photo snaps.

He's prepared as always for the cut, but not for how badly it burns this tim—a searing white flash there and gone so fast it leaves him breathless without quite understanding what just happened.

The dark-haired woman flinches and spins, her gaze passing over him as he pretends interest in La Joie de Vivre; Harney studies her when she turns away still searching.

She's younger than she looks in the photos, confirming his suspicion that she is untrained and reckless. In person, she also glows sleek and predatory with health, a difference so marked that it can't only be a matter of seeing her in real life. He thinks back through the photos he's seen of her, wondering if he will notice a positive progression in her health if he goes back through them in sequence.

But he's barely noticing her physical appearance, because what's missing is what intrigues him most. She's a void. The calm eye of a hurricane that whirls around them both—and if she wasn't so inexperienced she would surely feel the same thing from him.

She may not know what he is, but she can obviously sense something went wrong. She scans the crowd around her once more, unease sketching lines between her brows, then pulls her coat tighter and stalks away.

Harney follows her to a nearby Indian restaurant, slipping through the crowds with years of experience blending into the background. He stands in the shadow of an alley as she stabs her key distractedly at the door beside the restaurant's entrance, waits until she glares out her third-story window a moment later. She twitches the curtains shut.

Should he knock? Should he have spoken to her back when the photo was taken?

Harney isn't shy, he makes small talk with strangers all the time. But talking with her won't be an airy, bland conversation about the weather—she shares something with him that he didn't think any other person could.

And Harney, who can identify the most complex human emotions by taste like the most sophisticated perfumer, doesn't know what to call the sharp, resiny churn of sweet almond and capsaicin he's feeling.

Hope-desire-anticipation.

Jealousy-envy-resentment.

Terror.

He's so caught up in his own thoughts that it takes time for the panicked screams around him to spike through his awareness. A man has fainted a few meters away, and Harney suddenly realizes how overfull he is with the red pepper and vinegar anxiety the man had been carrying about telling his son he just lost his job. It roils in Harney's gut and he stumbles away, breaking the connection only seconds before he sips the man's final breaths.

The man gasps, coughing color back into his chalky face.

Harney locks himself in his hotel room, pacing and nauseous for hours until he finally loses the taste of the man's emotions. He hasn't lost control since he was young, and he'd never let it go so far, the emotions pouring into him like a funnel's been shoved down his throat.

When he studies himself in the mirror now, though, his complexion seems clearer, the lines that have been gathering around his eyes erased. His sclera are bright white, his fingernails a younger man's healthy pink.

Harney falls asleep well after midnight, skin clammy and cold under piles of blankets. He needs the perfect emotion to put him back on track. Something comfortable and predictable—a little sweet, a little bitter.

He slips into the Hinojosas' living room.

The entire family is dead, sprawled out in their usual favorite chairs, pale and drained with trickles of blood seeping from nostrils or tear ducts.

In her frame across the room, the dark-haired woman's cheeks are flushed, her lips plump from gorging. She meets his gaze, and she smiles.

She's not at her apartment the next morning.

She's not at the Trocadero.

She's not at Notre-Dame.

He retraces his favorite tourist haunts all over the City of

Light until his feet ache and his head is swimming from the sickly smorgasbord of sentiments. He finally collapses at a table at La Maison Rose, exhausted. It's late, the good light of the golden hour gone, the selfie seekers flocking to other parts of the city to document the trip.

"You prefer this place?"

Harney turns to greet the server, but instead of a bored youth at the end of their shift, it's the dark-haired woman.

He's been searching for her all day without a clear understanding of what he would do when he found her. *Stop her.* But stop her from invading his own hunting grounds? From killing? From eliciting the strange, complicated brew of feelings that uncoil deep within his gut when he thinks about the fact that someone else understands him?

Her cheeks are rosy, her eyes bright with the sort of glassy intensity he associates with those whose overriding emotion is a cloying *need-craving-obsession* for a thing they can no longer control their consumption of.

She sets two glasses of wine on the table in front of Harney and sits.

"You have been hunting a very long time," she says. "That gives me hope, I worried I would begin to get bored."

"You killed them."

The dark-haired woman lifts a languid shoulder. "Were they special to you? It is so fascinating to me that you go back time and time again."

"Why did you kill them?"

"You don't enjoy the final taste?"

"No. Of course not."

She tilts her head, a dark curl slipping off her shoulder. "You've never tried it."

"I'm not a monster."

"Suit yourself." She holds up her wine glass to him, and after a moment of hesitation he touches the lip of his glass to hers with a crystal chime. He barely tastes the cool, metallic liquid as it spills over his tongue. "But haven't you ever wondered what it's like?"

"No."

"Liar." Her laugh is melodic, sharp. "I saw you yesterday with the man in the alley. Trying to drink him dry."

"That was an accident."

"What did it feel like?"

He doesn't have to answer her. He doesn't want to go down this road, he finds himself confused by the *desire-fear-envy-hope* welling up below his sternum, the most complicated blend of emotions he has ever felt himself. Either, over the years, he has made himself an empty sponge to soak up the wine and vinegar others carelessly bleed out, or his condition created that empty place inside of him. He doesn't remember which it is anymore.

All he knows is that for the first time in years he feels something all his own.

He thinks of the families he collected, the thousands of threads of connection he always believed weave him into a community, each point tethered to a picture frame somewhere around this globe. He understands them far better than they will ever understand themselves. But not a single one of them knows his name. Not a single one of them has ever studied their vacation photos and wondered who the man in the background is, whether he has his own crushing joys or sweeping dreads.

"It felt like . . . drowning."

She lays her hand over his, and he feels nothing from her. No overwhelming crush of salty, sweet, caustic, floral, piquant that only leaves him hungrier then when he first tasted it. Right now, sensation comes from within, rather than without. And he feels satisfied.

"What's your name?" he asks.

"Madeleine," she answers.

"I'm Harney."

The corner of her blood-red lips curls into a playful smile.

"Hello, Harney. Where are you going next?"

GROVE

Erik Grove is a writer, long distance runner, and little dog wrangler doing things in Portland, OR. He enjoys tacos, robots, and using italics for emphasis. He is a guest host of the Overcast speculative fiction podcast. He has upcoming short fiction in ESCAPE POD and other places like his Mom's refrigerator. He'd definitely like to give you a hug or high five when this is all over.

You can find him on Twitter @erikgrove where he occasionally tweets dog photos, marathon training nonsense, and sundry writerly shenanigans. You can also check out his webpage www.erikgrove.com for fun and prizes!*

*There is no fun. There are no prizes. BUT there is cool content sometimes!

"Whispers" is the closest thing to a hug and high five I can offer you while we're still socially distancing in this Zoom Situation. I'm scared too but we can do this together. We're fucking unstoppable.

KWAK

Jessie Kwak is a freelance writer and novelist living in Portland, Oregon. She writes sci-fi and fantasy with a liberal dose of explosions, gunfights, and dinner parties. She likes to make her readers laugh. She is the author of supernatural thriller *Shifting Borders* and the *Durga System* series of gangster sci-fi stories.

You can learn more about her at www.jessiekwak.com, or follow her on Twitter (@jkwak) or Instagram (@kwakjessie).

Every time I travel to a popular tourist spot, I find myself dodging photo ops and wondering whose albums I'm inadvertently joining as a Background Street Crosser. I haven't discovered the ability to visit to their homes via those photos . . . yet.

McCOLLOUGH

Andrew McCollough writes science fiction, fantasy, and undecipherable scribbles. Mostly the latter. His work tends to describe unfortunate things happening to relatable protagonists and often involve magic or robots. He is the author of *Mermaid's Garden* and other short stories and his work is available at Grievous Angel and Amazon.

You can learn more about him at his website: www.andrewmccollough.com.

If you enjoyed "Blue Light" and want novel updates and freebie flash fiction, then join Andrew's mailing list by downloading a free copy of "The Mermaid's Garden."

https://dl.bookfunnel.com/fhx4089cpt

RISTAU

Kate Ristau is the author of the middle grade series, *Clockbreakers*, and the young adult series, *Shadow Girl*. You can read her essays in *The New York Times* and *The Washington Post*. In her ideal world, magic and myth combine to create memorable stories with unforgettable characters. Until she finds that world, she'll live in a house in Oregon, where they found a sword behind the water heater and fairies in the backyard.

You can follow her online at KateRistau.com.

Throughout the pandemic, I've relied on Zoom to connect me with my friends and family, but I started to wonder: what if no one was waiting on the other side? This story took me down that road, through love and loss and memory. But as my co-authors pointed out, my memory is, well, quite mushy at times. Is it seven degrees of Kevin Bacon or six? Was Christian Slater in *Tremors*? What happened in the first level of *GoldenEye*?

For me, the specifics weren't as important as the people and the experiences I had with them. This continues to be true in all of my writing: the stories matter, and the people we tell them to and tell them for are our most important audience.

That's why you'll find me writing middle grade and young adult beside memoir and adult fantasy; I look for the story, and the person who needs it the most.

I hope you find your own Zoom connection this year, and that there is always someone on your screen, or waiting somewhere down the line for you.

SHERRILL

Jeb R. Sherrill has an oddly disjointed background. Having stumbled through everything from performing stage magic and kinetic juggling on French television and in Las Vegas casinos, to teaching martial arts and circus techniques, to competitive sabre fencing, film and stage acting, dance, songwriting, and his ongoing stint as a popular YouTube personality, Jeb has the ADD of a 10 year old. Writing, however, has remained his greatest passion since early childhood, having also written a barrage of short stories and poetry.

Pinning down his style is difficult, however. His liquid, psychotropic images, philosophical undertones and pure unabashed strangeness have made fans across the Fantasy and Science Fiction spectrum. Best known for insane worlds, over the top characters and sometimes heady subject matter, his work may not be for the faint of heart, but reading it is always an adventure. He considers himself to be a fantasticst and a writer of fairy tales for adults.

Gary and Rick also appear in "The Garage," which you check out on YouTube. Recorded at the Rose City Book Pub, in fact.

https://www.youtube.com/watch?v=dSPkJvfJH5E

TEPPO

Mark Teppo divides his time between Portland and Sumner, and he tends to navigate by local bookstore positioning. He writes historical fiction, fantasy, speculative fiction, and horror, and has published more than a dozen novels. If he's writing a mystery, he's pretending to be Harry Bryant.

He also runs Underland Press, an independent publishing house.

You can learn more about him at www.markteppo.com, or follow him on Twitter or Instagram (@markteppo).

The title of this story is pronounced "The Message in the Medium." If you've enjoyed this story, you should sign up for my newsletter, where I regularly update everyone on what I'm working on, what records I've been listening to, and what board games I've been playing.

http://www.markteppo.com/mailing-list

More Cocaine

Naturally, we have to flog the drug metaphor well past its usefulness, so here's one more for you.

The first one was, well, it's wasn't *free* free, but it was mostly—okay, *sorta* free. And we know you probably want more. At least we hope you do, and so to be all helpful and accommodating, we've got a sign-up form at our website.

Yes, there's a website, and if the URL didn't self-present itself, here you go:

http://www.spacecocaine.com

Plug your email address into the appropriate form, and we'll notify you when the next shipment of **SPACE COCAINE** is imminent. That way you can plan your budgets and recreational time accordingly.

You're welcome.

Fancy Doodle Page

Space Cocaine 2 premiered at the Rose City Book Pub in Portland, OR, on June 1st, 2021. Some of us were in attendance because we had social distanced for a year, gotten our shots, and done our duties as respectful citizens of this planet. If there are signatures on this page, then you managed to accomplish the same self-sacrifice. Good for you.

www.ingramcontent.com/pod-product-compliance
Lightning Source LLC
Chambersburg PA
CBHW050421110726
47899CB00008B/2800